THE

TOPPLING

TOWERS

Barbara Willard

BARBARA WILLARD

*With love
To
Julia*

*21st April
'69*

LONGMANS YOUNG BOOKS

LONGMANS YOUNG BOOKS LTD
London and Harlow
Associated companies, branches and representatives
throughout the world

SBN 582 15842 7

Printed in Great Britain by
C. Tinling & Co. Ltd
Liverpool, London and Prescot

THE TOPPLING TOWERS

Contents

1   News of a Distant Tower   11

2   The Towering Plans   23

3   A Tower Returns   35

4   The Stranger   47

5   The Toppling   62

6   Towers in Trouble   75

7   Mostly Anthea   88

8   Unauthorised Persons   103

9   Old Cars, Young Towers   118

10   Oliver   135

11   The Tokens   147

THE TOPPLING TOWERS

Important

This book is a continuation of the story begun in *The Family Tower*. That first book is concerned with the arrival of Emily, an unknown young cousin from Africa, where she was born, and where her parents have been killed in a car crash, her gradual absorption into the huge Tower family, and her acceptance into their game called 'Family Tower', whose meetings are known as 'Towerings'.

The Towers have lived in and around Milsom Parva in Dorset ever since Great-grandfather William started a small cycle repair shop near the bridge. That small beginning has blossomed into Tower Motors Ltd, a rich and prosperous concern with immense works and smart showrooms in the town. All the branches of the family are concerned in Tower Motors, but the young Towers intend to be particularly involved. Unlike their parents, they are not interested in seats on the Board or administrative jobs. They want to be mechanics, designers, test drivers—not only the boys, but the girls.

By the time *The Family Tower* ends much has happened to a lot of people as a result of Emily's arrival—and uneasiness is growing about Tower Motors. Perhaps it is not quite as safe and steady as might be supposed . . . Perhaps these Towers could topple . . .

News of a Distant Tower

A FEW days after Christmas the telephone bell rang in the David Towers' house and Jo answered. It was her cousin, Sukey Miller, which made Jo sigh a little. Sukey these holidays had been rather a trial to them all, but particularly to Jo. Always inclined to exaggerate, Sukey at the moment was changing her hair style every other day, borrowing clothes, using curious make-up and needing constant flattery to keep her going.

'Guess what?' cried Sukey now, almost screaming down the wire. 'Guess what? Guess what?'

'Do you mean three guesses?'

'It'll take you more than three.'

'I'm just going out,' said Jo falsely. 'Need it take so long?' In fact she was almost sure she knew already what Sukey had to tell her.

'Anthea's coming home!' shrieked Sukey.

Jo was silent, stunned. This was not what she had expected. 'Truly?' she said at last.

'Truly, truly!' Sukey's voice changed, it crumpled. 'My own sister—and I haven't seen her for three years. Suppose she comes home speaking American?'

'I expect she will ... You're not crying, are you?'

'Yes, I am. She won't know me. I shan't know her. We'll be strangers. We may not even like one another. I wish she wasn't coming.'

'Well, dear me,' said Jo, her thoughts in some confusion. She disapproved of Anthea—how *could* she have turned her back on the family Tower?—but none the less she had always seemed a prodigy of boldness and bravery, whatever her reasons for departing. 'Oh lor', Sukey—can't you blow your nose or something?'

'It won't make it any better if I do.'

'It'll sound better.'

'I wish she wasn't coming *just now*. Anyway, it's been all right without her.'

'Just now? Oho—do you mean what I think you mean?'

'Yes, of course I do.' Sukey had started shrieking again. 'Daddy and Margaret are getting married at last. It'll all be spoilt if Anthea turns up and makes scenes.'

'Why should she?' Jo was feeling a pleasant sentimental glow at the confirmation of all their hopes. Uncle Brian Miller deserved to be made happy again, and they all, even Aunt Harriet, liked the self-effacing Margaret Dale. 'Sukey—I'm frightfully glad about Uncle Brian. Aren't you all pretty excited?'

'I don't want Anthea to come spoiling it all. She writes to Daddy regularly once a month—all about nothing—always the same ending, "I'm fine. No need to worry. Coming home one day." '

'Well, then—she said she'd come and she's coming . . . Look out—you're going to cry again!'

Sukey, indeed, was already weeping. 'I keep thinking how Anthea went away when Mummy died because she couldn't bear anyone to take her place in the house. But I *want* Daddy and Margaret to get married. So that makes me a terrible treacherous traitor.'

'As to why Anthea went away,' Jo said brutally, 'there are two opinions, aren't there? They do say she couldn't bear to take on the job of housekeeper and nursemaid to all you lot.'

'You sound like Aunt Harriet or someone . . .'

'I didn't say I blamed her, did I? I suppose she knows about Uncle Brian and Margaret? Then she's coming home because it's safe. No one can land her with the job of little mother now.'

'You're so clinical it isn't true.'

'If you mean cynical, by any chance . . . Well, anyway—what do the others think about it all?'

It appeared that the Miller twins, Hugh and Robin, were overjoyed about both bits of news. The little sisters, Penny and Rachel, had been told about Anthea but were supposed to know nothing about the coming marriage.

'Of course they do know, really,' Sukey said. 'They're keen.'

Jo laughed. Rachel seemed a bit young to be keen, but it was a good word for Penny, who had a rather sharp inquisitive manner, like a self-possessed mouse.

'I'm keen, too,' Jo said. 'Margaret's been one of us for ages— or she could have been if she wasn't so jolly careful not to push. Now she's the *vraie chose*, as Oliver's bound to say. I think you're lucky. And I don't see why you need to moan about Anthea. Actually, you're going to have two new relations all at once.'

'Yes, I suppose so,' Sukey agreed, sounding a lot more cheerful. 'Yes, I am, aren't I?'

'Anthea's bound to have lots of super clothes you can borrow.'

'That reminds me—would you lend me your white turtle-neck sweater for the weekend?'

'No,' said Jo; and hung up on her cousin's wails.

As she turned away from the telephone, Roland came down the stairs, nodding his head in an approving way.

'Tied it all up at last, then, have they?'

'Who?' asked Jo stonily.

'Oh come off it, Jo. I just happened to be passing Ma's bed-room when the phone bell rang. Naturally I answered it.'

'And naturally you settled down to enjoy the conversation as soon as you knew it was a private matter.'

'Naturally, naturally,' said Roland, grinning. 'Anyway—what's private about Uncle Brian and Margaret? We've all known it would happen eventually. As for the other item—no one's going to keep that quiet for long, are they?'

'Do you remember Anthea?'

'Just about. I wasn't quite one of the tinies when she went. It's only two or three years, dear—or correct me if I'm wrong.'

It was Jo's turn to grin. Roland was growing up. He had caught some tricks from the admired Miller twins, who were both rather smooth and sophisticated after their year working in the showroom of Tower Motors, followed by a first term at Cambridge . . . Their sister Anthea was older than they were. It would be odd for Hugh and Robin, accustomed to being the eldest Millers, when she returned. A lot had happened in three years. Some of it was on the surface, purely factual—like the marriage of their cousin Camilla; like the arrival from Ghana of the unknown Emily, her parents both killed in a car crash. But some of it was subtle and concealed —like the shift in relationships throughout the family, the result of time and circumstance—like the way Jo and Roland, a comfortable family of two, had turned with surprising success into a family of three, Jo, Roland and Emily. But there were other things, less happy, for Anthea to learn about when she came home to her own people. How impossible, how nonsensical it had seemed to Jo last summer when her Uncle Saville hinted at some threat to Tower Motors. Now, half a year later, they all knew the menace to be real. *All our lives could be changed,* she had said to herself on waking, the day after her father had explained to her how the family business might be taken over by the huge company called County Mechanical Holdings. And she had stuck her face into the pillow and felt herself shrivel in rage and fear, her pride beating in her ears like a heavy pulse. What would they do, where would they go, the Towers who had almost built the town of Milsom Parva into what it was today, if the family business ceased to exist?

'Where's Emily?' she asked Roland now, as he leant against the banisters, trying to unscrew a small bottle.

'We're cleaning up your collection.'

'I didn't say you could,' cried Jo, but without much conviction —she liked to keep the collection of model cars under her own control, but it was lovely to have the cleaning done for her.

'Emily thought it would be a nice surprise.'

'It is a surprise.'

'A nice one,' he insisted. 'I came down to use an opener on this bottle of oil.'

'What sort of oil?' She was very suspicious.

'The right sort, of course,' said Roland. At that moment the cap moved and he said 'Ah' and dashed back up the stairs again.

'Be careful!' Jo shouted after him. 'The wheels come off very easily.'

'I've noticed.'

'I don't want any of them lost!'

'Hush, dear,' he said. He vanished along the landing and a door opened. Jo heard Emily say something impatient, eager. Roland gave his chortling laugh. Then the door banged.

Jo stood where he had left her, feeling vaguely neglected. She wished she had one of her favourite cousins, Lydia Holt or Oliver Evens at hand. She wished her mother was at home, but she and Auntie Jay Cardew had gone for the day to London. Jo felt curiously empty-handed as she stood still at the bottom of the stairs, knowing Emily and Roland were amusing themselves together, though truly for her benefit.

The Christmas holidays were almost over. They had been especially good holidays. There had been a wonderful Christmas Day party at the Robert Towers', the best Jo could remember. Camilla had come home, rather smugly plump because of the baby due in April, and Alan had seemed more than ever the ideal husband. But perhaps most of all it was Emily's absorption into the family that had made the whole season doubly satisfying to Jo. Perhaps they had all expected that this first Christmas without her parents would upset Emily; but she had taken it in her stride, and she and Jo had now a cosy sort of joke calling one another 'sister'—though only when there was an audience to laugh. Neither of them remembered which had started this, but it had set a seal on an important development. Now it was as though Emily, who might, as Oliver had once said, be either ten or a hundred years old, had learned in the months she had been with them to grow to her true age. Jo saw her mother's pleasure in this and knew that she herself had cleared the first really difficult hurdle of her life.

The end of the holidays meant a general break-up of the cousins. The two at boarding-school, Oliver and Sukey, would vanish this time next week. Rose would be back for her second year at the Technical College at Barhampton—Clive had finished and was now at the works—and Tamsin would drive in each day with Rose to be dropped at the nearby Art School. At home in Milsom would be Jo and Roland and Emily, and the young twins, Martin and Simon Evens. The senior twins, the Millers, Hugh and Robin, at present away ski-ing, would be home only a day or two before going back to the university for their second term. If only they could all be in Milsom Parva, every one of them all the time, Jo felt, the combined power of the family would surely save Tower Motors from falling into alien hands. She was full of sympathy for demonstrators in this cause or that, who threw themselves down in the street to obstruct events—for that was exactly what she felt like doing herself.

Jo was relieved that Emily was to remain at school in Milsom. There had been a lot of talk about her going off to boarding-school with Sukey, but plans had been changed. This had caused some rather brisk correspondence between Jo's father and Emily's American aunt, a trustee though not a guardian. However, it was not to please Jo that these arrangements had been made. It was because the plans for Kojo Amponsah to come to England from Ghana had suddenly matured. Kojo's parents and Emily's had been close friends, so obviously it would be madness to bring him over in order to please Emily—and then to send her away to school.

Jo had thought of Kojo's visit as being far in the future. But some part of the complicated negotiations that involved the Home Office and the Education Authority must have fallen neatly into a slot—and the rest had followed automatically. Kojo, who was now seventeen, was to spend a year at Tower Motors, a year at Barhampton College of Technology, and a third year back again with Tower Motors. No one had suggested that Tower Motors might not last that long, but a lot of them must have had uneasy secret thoughts of the kind.

'If Kojo's going to stay here,' Roland had said, 'he can have my room and I'll have the glory hole over the garage.'

'That's nice of you, Roland,' his mother said.

'Generous boy—he's been wanting it for years,' said Jo.

'I think it's a very good arrangement.' Deborah Tower looked at her husband—'What do you think, David?'

'You mean—will I get the glory hole painted at last? More work for the old man.'

Alone with her mother that evening, Jo found herself grumbling. 'This household keeps growing all the time.' Her feelings about the stranger were increasingly mixed, but chiefly she was frightened of him—or perhaps of her own weaknesses. Was she, in fact, capable of welcoming such a stranger?

'You didn't want Emily,' her mother reminded her.

'It's different,' said Jo, awkwardly because she did not want to say it. 'He's different.'

'And who, precisely, is the same?' Deborah asked her. 'I'm old and you're young, and Roland's a boy and Emily's a girl. We're all different.'

'He's *so* different, Mummy.'

'And we'll be *so different* to him, too. Don't forget that, will you? He'll need Emily to help him over his early days in England. He won't know any more about English life than we know about African. And we'll be on our own ground . . . What does worry me, though, is what will happen to Emily when she sees him.'

'Why . . . ? Yes—I know, I know what you mean. Of course I

do. Oh dear! Everything's so difficult. You mean Emily will remember about her parents and everything—it'll all be fresh again.'

'I'm afraid so. She's bound to be upset, poor child. I dread it.'

'She may not be,' Jo said slowly. 'I mean—I think she must know how she'll feel and she's not worried. So why should you be? Emily *knows* things, Mummy.'

Deborah did not reply to that. She tightened her mouth a little. Jo knew that none of the older members of the family wanted to believe in Emily's peculiar gift, something near to second sight. It was one of those moments when the generations divided sharply and Jo felt herself withdrawing impatiently from her mother.

When Jo and Lydia met at school on the first day of the spring term, they were able to discuss Anthea's return. Jo, a great maker of plans, had already decided what should be done to welcome her. The game of Family Tower, with its strict rules and regulations, its elected leader and its ability to gather them all, every single cousin, into one place at one time, might have been invented for the occasion.

'We must have a Towering, Lydia, and discuss how to arrange a welcome home. I know what I'd like us to do.'

'Take the whole Towering to the airport, I suppose,' Lydia said. 'It's a lovely idea. When is she due, do you know?'

'Sunday week, I think.'

'That means doing without Oliver and Sukey.'

'Oh Sukey'll get a day out because of greeting her long-lost sister. And Oliver's sure to manage something. He always does.'

'It's very strange to think about Anthea, Jo. She always seems such an exciting sort of person, though I don't really know why. I don't think I remember her very well. I don't know what I remember and what I've made up. Nobody knows what she's been doing all this time—Hugh and Robin always say she writes letters about nothing.'

'Perhaps she's married by now,' said Jo.

'Oh no.' Lydia was quite positive.

'You're always the same,' Jo complained. 'You think she'd be so deliriously happy she'd never be able to keep it to herself. You're so *soft*, Lydia. Perhaps she's keeping it to herself because she's bloody miserable.'

'Oh do shut up,' said Lydia uncomfortably. 'I hate you when you swear about the place.'

Jo laughed, but fondly. It was never much fun shocking Lydia because she was so easily hurt. 'Let's call a Towering, then, shall we?' she said, putting Anthea and swearing on one side for the time being.

'Have you spoken to High Tower?'

'Not yet. It'll be her first Towering. Shall I speak to her or will you?'

The never-omitted routine ran its brief course.

'You,' said Lydia . . .

Cleaning Jo's collection of model cars had taken longer than Roland or Emily had expected. They were at it again that evening and Jo found them both in her room when she got home from school. Keenly as she desired to have a Towering, Jo had had to steel herself to approach Emily, for this was the last difficulty that lay between them. Jo had to admit, wretchedly, that she was still not utterly resigned to the fact that Emily had been made High Tower, while she herself had been only the runner-up.

'Just the right moment,' said Emily. 'That's the lot.' She looked pleased with her work and her smile was free and cheerful. Since her arrival last spring her face had filled out and her pale skin coloured a little. 'Doesn't it look smashing?'

'Yes, it does. Thanks awfully . . . I would now like to discuss a matter of importance, High Tower.'

Emily stood wiping her hands slowly and methodically on an oily rag, like any mechanic—or like any reasonable member of the Tower family, Jo thought with satisfaction.

'Yes, Wish Tower? What matter of importance?'

'It's about our cousin Anthea . . .'

'Roland—I mean Saxon Tower—and I were just talking about her.'

'We think there should be some form of welcome, High Tower.'

'Yes,' agreed High Tower. 'A very good idea. To make real plans. To discuss suggestions . . . Is that what you mean?'

'Precisely.'

'Then please make the necessary arrangements, Wish Tower. Have you discussed it with Round Tower?'

'I have.'

'Then proceed, Wish Tower. Let's say next Sunday evening at Rose's flat. If she'll have us.'

Jo nodded her head, formally and solemnly—it was almost a bow. However much she might have to struggle over accepting Emily as High Tower, she was pleased that her young cousin was so entirely able to cope with the appointment. Indeed she felt proud of her.

The Towers would have been lost without telephones. Roland had once said that the bell rang with a Tower voice. Certainly it was a Tower voice that answered, at least eight times out of ten. That evening as Jo was clearing up before going to bed the voice was Uncle Robert's.

'I'm just going to bed,' said Jo, because Uncle Robert always flustered her.

'That need not worry me,' he replied. 'It's your father I want to speak to.'

'I didn't mean—' began Jo. Then wisely gave up further conversation. 'I'll fetch him, Uncle Robert.'

Her father was already coming out of the poky little room he called his study.

'Is it Robert?'

'Yes. Wants to speak to you . . .'

Her father strode across the hall and took the receiver from her almost roughly.

'Yes?' he said. 'Well? What happened?'

Jo turned away and went very slowly up the stairs. She sat on the top step with her knees hunched and her hands over her ears, trying not to listen. Her heart was thumping so hard that she felt sick. Something was happening—something horrible was happening. Uncle Saville's voice as she had heard it last summer echoed nastily through her mind: 'I suppose all towers can topple . . . even the Towers of Milsom Parva, Jo.'

Jo waited until she heard the ting of the bell that meant her father had hung up. Then she went fast down the stairs and called to him over the banisters.

'Daddy—is it something awful?'

'What's that? Oh Jo—I thought you'd gone to bed, my girl.'

'Is it Tower Motors?' she insisted. She moved down to the bottom step and sat there, and David Tower sat down beside her. 'Please tell me, Daddy. I'm in it, too. I am, really. We all are. You know that.'

'Nothing awful's happened yet, Jo. Just that it's come nearer. A take-over bid by C.M.H. You know what a take-over bid means?'

'Only sort-of. Buying up all the shares?'

'Offering the shareholders a better price. I don't think the present offer is really quite good enough to tempt many of them. Some, of course. The difficulty comes when the offer is so good that one can only advise one's shareholders to accept it—because we ourselves couldn't hope to do as well for them. Every company like ours has a responsibility to its shareholders.'

'I thought big companies were supposed to be rather wicked—capitalists and all that.'

'Oh,' he said, 'how difficult it all is! We live in a great period of transition and revolution, Jo. You can't start a company without shareholders' money—and that means the shareholders live on work done by other people. But sometimes they've worked for years themselves and invested their hard-won savings . . . This is why there's an argument for nationalisation, of course. The State would run everything . . . I'm in just as much of a muddle as you, Jo. I've reached the point of not knowing what's really good for us.'

'I always *think* I know what I think,' said Jo. 'But some days I want to get rid of the Royal Family, and other days I want to grind the faces of the workers. If ever there was a real revolution I should think I'd change sides every other day.'

'Let's see how we manage our own revolution, shall we? Your Uncle Robert's in a fine state. All very well for him—he's due for retirement, anyway, and he's got plenty to retire on. The rest of us . . . Well . . . Funny if your old man found himself out of a job.'

2

The Towering Plans

THE Towering was held the following Sunday, early in the evening. They went to the Cardews' house, where Rose, an only child, was indulged to the point of being allowed the whole of the top floor to herself. Rose's flat, it was called. The Cardews were the richest of the various branches of the family—richer than the Robert Towers. Great-aunt Mary Tower had married the only son of a wealthy industrialist; when he died she returned to Milsom Parva with her son, Peter, Rose's father—so he, like all the others, had become absorbed into Tower Motors. Following the precedent set by his mother, Peter Cardew had also married richly. His wife Jane, Auntie Jay, spent her own money with extreme generosity; any one of them in a tight corner would always ask her help. Jo knew to her shame that Uncle Saville, her mother's brother, so no Tower at all, had been helped by Auntie Jay at least once.

Rose Cardew was spoilt, so some of the aunts and uncles said. Certainly she had a great many possessions that her various cousins would be happy to own—but she was casual and easy about all this. The enormous room at the top of the house was the one thing of Rose's that Jo coveted. The ceiling sloped and the windows poked out over the roof, opening up a view across the town to the countryside. You could see over the buildings of Tower Motors to the river beyond, where it slid strongly under the bridge that carried the main road. At night the lights on the bridge arched and reflected, and where the newer building was scrambling up the far hillside the sweep of crescents and the tidy boxes of squares were picked out in perforated lines of light.

Up on this top floor of the house Rose had not only the big low room that she called her studio, but also a small bedroom and a bathroom with an indulgent-looking primrose bath. She also had such things as an electric toaster, a coffee mill and an electric percolator, and jars full of various kinds of coffee bean, about which she was rather vain and snobbish. There was a fine smell of brewing coffee as the Towering began to muster. They were all to be there, since Hugh and Robin Miller had returned from Austria the previous night. 'I only just got Hugh on the plane,' Robin had said earlier that day. 'He was enmeshed with a girl.' The Miller twins had arrived at Rose's with their two little sisters, Penny and Rachel, piled into the back of the Spitfire. Clive came in his old Morris with Lydia, collecting Jo, Roland and Emily on the way. Tamsin Tower and Sukey Miller chose to walk, while the three Evens boys got a lift with Auntie Jay and Uncle Peter Cardew, who had conveniently been visiting at the Evens home. Oliver muttered privately to Jo that he was ashamed of being seen anywhere near the Cardews' vast car, and Martin and Simon said the springing was so magnificent it had made them feel sick.

'A lot of you will have to sit on the floor,' Rose said, throwing cushions about. 'The coffee's almost ready. I'm sorry the cups are so mixed. You sit here, Sukey. Oliver—shove the sofa against the wall—make a bit more room. You share with Penny, Rachel.' Penny looked gloomy at this, for she always had to put up with Rachel. 'Are you okay, Jo? Move up a bit, Clive, and let Tamsin sit there. Lydia, be a duck and give me a hand with the coffee. Martin and Simon—sit down and shut up.' She ordered them about quietly, in her light, deceptively gentle voice. Her small, apparently frail hands flapped absurdly.

'Look at her,' Clive said. 'You'd think she was only fit for picking flowers.'

'Or playing the harpsichord,' said Tamsin. 'But you should have seen her taking down Uncle Brian's old Rover the other day.'

Clive grinned. 'She's got a grip like a vice, and I'm sorry to say she knows more about mechanics than I'm ever going to.'

'Do you want sugar?' Rose was asking. 'Then come and fetch it, Clive.' And the hands with a grip like a vice gracefully offered him a small delicate silver sugar bowl. 'What are we going to discuss, High Tower?' she asked Emily, who had seated herself on a round, revolving piano stool in the middle of the floor.

'Wish Tower and Round Tower know about the business of the meeting,' Emily said austerely. The Towering was not supposed to discuss the current matter except in proper session, and they had not been called to order yet.

Rose smiled at Emily's very correct reply and tried to trip her. 'It's about Anthea, I suppose. I'd love to know why she's coming home. Do you think it's just because of the wedding?'

Emily shrugged and said nothing, and Rose gave it up and turned away to speak to one of the others.

Jo and Lydia were sitting on the floor in a corner, talking amiably and aimlessly together. The wonderful Christmas had eased away the last tiny remnant of Lydia's resentment about the part Emily had come to play in Jo's life. They were as comfortable together now as they had been ever since they could remember.

The noise was considerable. There were fifteen of them and the room was low-pitched. Soon they had all to shout to make themselves heard. Robin turned up the volume of the record player because he could hardly hear even the rather booming symphony he had chosen. Hugh was describing, with generous gestures and enthusiastic cries in peculiar German, how he had almost won a ski race at the close of the holiday. Cups were clattering on saucers, spoons tinkling, and Tamsin and Sukey were arguing hotly about clothes.

'I've simply changed my line, that's all,' Tamsin cried. 'If I want to look like a balloonist—and that's your idea, not mine—then I'll look that way and you can like it. In fact, I've decided to design exclusively *motor* clothes from now on. I don't believe anybody ever has and I intend to open my own boutique next door to the showrooms. And even if I never learn to drive and can't tell a distributor from a frying pan, I shall still be as much a part of the firm as any of you smart engineering types.'

'You're quite right, Tam,' Oliver said. 'It is a good idea. How soon will you be able to get at it?'

'Well, I've only done six months at the Art School—' Tamsin began—which made all the older ones burst into cruel laughter. 'All right. Laugh. I don't care. I know what I know.'

'Ignore them,' Oliver said. 'Three years or so from now I'll be ordering my specially designed overalls from Tam Tower's boutique. A nice print, I think—spanners cunningly entwined—dark blue on a yellow ground.'

'Laugh away, my dears,' said Tamsin, glowering.

'Funny thing is,' Oliver told her, 'I'm not laughing. You might make a fortune.'

Three years from today, Oliver had said. Jo had heard him because she always heard Oliver, however much family row was going on around them. Three years from today—where would Tower Motors be? Where would they all be? And this second question struck her forcibly as being the answerable one of the two. They would be where they had always meant to be—working for Tower Motors even if it was Tower Motors no longer, Tower Motors in disguise. And if those who took over Tower Motors refused to employ members of the Tower family —then the young Towers would start again where Great-grandfather William Tower had started and build a new world of their own. They would do it quicker, too, for there had only been one of him and there were lots of them ... The simplicity of it astounded her. She seemed to see exactly where she and all the rest of them were going ...

'Jo,' Rose was saying. 'Hi—*Jo!* Lydia—give her a sharp tap.'

'Jo,' said Lydia, nudging her gently.

'Mm?' said Jo.

'Time we started—isn't it?'

It was high time. The boys collected the coffee cups, Robin turned off the player. A moderate quiet spread over the room, the young Towers began sorting themselves out, drifting into a pattern that was usual without being obligatory—Jo and Lydia side by side, as the originators of Family Tower and the convenors of all meetings; the two pairs of twins together; Sukey with the little sisters; Tamsin next to Rose, then Clive on her other side; Oliver across from Jo so that they could more easily exchange significant glances if the business of the meeting, or its conduct, seemed to call for them. Roland was the only one who drifted about a bit, seeming uncertain where it would be best for him to settle. Usually he liked to be with the older twins, but today he chose one of the girls, folding up on the floor near Tamsin.

'I don't think you look like a balloonist,' he assured her. 'I think you look smashing.'

'Could be I *want* to look like a balloonist,' said Tamsin rather tartly . . .

'Time to start,' Jo said to Lydia. 'You do it.'

'No, you,' said Lydia as usual.

Jo stood up. 'Is everybody ready?'

'Ready,' they answered solemnly.

Jo bowed to Emily, who was still sitting on the round piano stool in the centre of the room. 'Then I call upon High Tower to produce the Token and declare a Towering.'

'Here is the Token,' said High Tower. She held out her hand with the little gold tower lying in the palm. 'Thank you, Wish Tower and Round Tower. Pronounce the business of the Towering.'

In the now quiet room, with Rose's carefully dramatic lighting adding atmosphere, High Tower's young firm voice was impressive. Although this was her first appearance as High Tower, not one of them doubted her ability to carry it off without prompting. Her choice of words alone inspired confidence. *Pronounce* the business. Others had most often said merely, 'What is the business?' or, 'What is the first item on the agenda?' just as though this was any old committee meeting instead of the traditional council of the young Towers.

'The business of the Towering,' said Wish Tower, 'is to discuss plans for a returning Tower.'

'The sister of Watch Tower, Clock Tower, Bell Tower and the two Turrets,' said Martello Tower, helpfully, from his place opposite.

'Yes—she is the Tower returning,' agreed Wish Tower, giving him a glance of appreciation. *The Tower returning* sounded good, too—almost poetic, as words often are when cunningly or unexpectedly delivered in reverse order. There was little doubt that today's Towering was getting off to a very good start.

'When does she come? And how? And why?' asked High Tower. She spun on her piano stool and faced Clock Tower and Watch Tower. 'Let the brothers speak,' she commanded.

They were almost twice her age. This might have been a moment for the Family Tower to rock on its foundations, blown by a gale of laughter. But so closely did this long-founded invention hold and bind them that there was no slightest hint of mockery in the brothers' reply.

'When? Next Sunday.'

'How? By charter flight to London.'

'Why?' Bell Tower shrugged. 'We don't precisely know.'

'A wedding . . . ?' Wish Tower prompted.

'The letters crossed. Hers came before she got the news.'

There was a mild sensation at this, but somebody said surely a Tower could return to her family without having any particular reason or excuse?

High Tower twirled on the piano stool and came to rest in her original place.

'Wish Tower—'

'Yes, High Tower?'

'The returning Tower should be welcomed.' She waited for the sounds of approval to die down. 'I commend that each Tower in turn suggests how best to celebrate a Tower's return.'

'Is it agreed?' Wish Tower asked the Towering.

'Agreed.'

With that they settled down to business.

The Towering plans were supposed to be kept secret, but something leaked out. Jo was at Eason Elms with the Holts on the Saturday before Anthea was due. It was Lydia's mother, Ruth Holt, who said doubtfully, 'Don't you think Uncle Brian will want to meet her alone?'

A deathly silence followed this bombshell. Jo, Lydia, Clive looked at one another helplessly.

'No one thought of that,' Lydia said. She looked desperately at her mother. 'What are we going to do now?'

'Perhaps I'm quite wrong,' Ruth said. 'But I think you should say something to Uncle Brian.'

'None of the others said anything against it,' Clive objected. 'Surely Hugh or Robin . . . Well, they're pretty responsible and he's their father and she's their sister.'

'We've made such plans,' Jo said gloomily. 'The whole Towering's going to be there. Gilbert's lent us his old Hillman and that'll make a fourth car so that no one need be left out.'

'Yes, I know. If it hadn't been for that I might not have known anything about it.'

'Surely he didn't *tell* you?' Jo cried. She would have trusted Gilbert, the foreman at Tower Motors, with her darkest secrets.

'Well, poor dear, he didn't realise I wasn't in on the business. I happened to be in with the car for servicing and he said something about sprucing it up to go to London Airport.'

'He should have known,' Clive said. 'Still—perhaps it's just as well. We'll just have to make some alterations. Uncle Brian could meet Anthea and we could do the reception committee stuff in the car park or somewhere. Then he can drive her home.'

'Ask him,' Ruth insisted. 'If your father was meeting you after three years, Lydia, he wouldn't want the whole family whooping around.'

Her choice of words made Clive hoot with laughter, and Lydia joined in, but rather faintly because she was watching Jo's black face.

Jo was boiling with rage and frustration. She had cycled over to the Holt's farm immediately after breakfast, simply so that she could go over the arrangements with Clive and Lydia, and now she got on her bicycle and started for home again. But Clive headed her off at the corner where the lane ran by one of the farm field gates, and Lydia came panting up only seconds behind him.

'We must decide what to do,' Clive said.

'Don't speak to me,' Jo cried, trying to shove past him, and picking crossly at his fingers gripping the handlebars. But he hung on.

'Don't be such a mug, Jo. We're not going to waste all these glorious plans. They'll have to be rearranged.'

'Like how?' grunted Jo.

'We can speak to Uncle Brian, for a start,' Lydia said.

There was a telephone box half a mile down the road, where three lanes crossed at a triangle of grass. They moved off in that direction, Jo pedalling slowly and the other two making haste beside her. It was better for them than for her, for the morning was bitter, frost still in the hedges and a slight fog holding the trees shrouded. At last the three of them were squeezed into the phone box and arguing about who should do the talking.

'You, Clive,' Lydia said. 'You can use a manly line.'

'He likes girls,' Clive objected.

'He might be afraid of offending us. You do it.'

Five minutes later they were all three careering down the lane in a state of jubilation. 'To tell you the truth,' Brian Miller had said, 'I'm frightened out of my wits at the idea of meeting Anthea after all this time. You'll be most valuable. You can take care of the few minutes after the first greeting, and by the time I'm driving her home on my own—the ice will be broken.'

'He sounded so *relieved!*' said Clive.

'He's nice,' Lydia said. 'Isn't he, Jo? Oh I do hope he'll be wildly happy with Margaret.'

'Why shouldn't he be?' Jo was being provocative, but as she spoke she remembered about such things as shareholders' meetings, and how her father had told her one would be called shortly.

'Last minute check-up,' Clive was saying. 'Jo—who's getting the flowers?'

'Tamsin. It's going to be madly expensive at this time of year.'

'Oh anyone'll give credit to Uncle Robert's daughter ...' Lydia cried. Then broke off, and looked at the other two. It was the nearest any of them had yet come to speaking about the rumblings of trouble in Tower Motors. In the quick, troubled glance that Clive exchanged with Jo there was the beginning of a new partnership—they had been far more in sympathy since last summer's rally at Milsom Magnificorum, though the long habit of bickering between them died hard.

Jo cycled home in a rather variable mood. She was delighted with the plans for next day, with the elaborate ceremonial they had, as members of the Towering, arranged for the occasion. If only Tamsin could get enough flowers it would be wonderful. And how splendid for Anthea to come home and find them all with arms outstretched to greet her and hug her back into the family fold. She did not choose to remind herself that Anthea had quitted the fold by choice and that she had cut herself off, more or less, ever since. Jo preferred to think that Anthea was also returning of her own free-will. It stood to reason, therefore, in Jo's firm vision of Tower domestic politics, that Anthea was coming back to England, Milsom Parva and her family because she could no longer bear to live separated from them ...

There was a lot of noise going on indoors as Jo swished through the gate and rammed her bike to a standstill against the rockery. She could hear her mother laughing, and Emily's voice high with excitement; and Roland kept saying the same thing over and over again, because quite obviously no one was listening to him.

Jo dashed up the steps and banged through the front door—and there they all were in the hall, Emily, Roland, both the parents; so whatever had happened had happened to them there—which seemed to suggest a telephone call.

'Jo!' cried Emily. 'Guess!'

'I'm always being told to guess lately. All right—I guess you've heard from Kojo.'

'You're not even surprised!' Emily complained, as everyone burst out laughing. 'Anyway—you haven't guessed *when*.'

'When . . . ? Oh *no*! I think I have guessed, after all . . .'

'Tomorrow!' Emily was almost transparent with excitement, Jo said afterwards, telling all this to Oliver.

'Where? What time? Is he coming to London?'

'Of course he is. And about half an hour later than Anthea! Isn't it staggering and stunning, Jo? We shall all be there to meet him. The whole Towering. We can just move on from Anthea to Kojo.'

Jo said—'Not as a Towering, though.'

'Why not?'

'He's not a Tower.'

'What difference does that make?'

'You're High Tower,' Jo said, 'so you ought to know. Of course we can all meet him, if you think that's what he'd like. But we'll just have to be us, not the Towering.'

'Talk about it later,' said her mother rather quickly.

'That's right, isn't it, Roland?' Jo insisted.

'Yes, I'm sure it is,' agreed Roland, though he would rather have given in and pleased Emily.

For the first time since she had come to live with them, David Tower saw his niece Emily looking angry. She lost her colour and her face seemed to fold in on itself, her eyes narrowing and her mouth tightening.

32

'I know what you mean,' she said, in a small chilly voice. 'I know what you're thinking.'

'Now, Emily—Emily dear—' cried Deborah Tower.

'I know what you think I'm thinking,' Jo snapped. 'As it happens *I'm not!*'

She shouted the last two words, and her father told her sharply and shortly to be quiet.

'It's because he's an African,' said Emily. 'What makes you think white people are so marvellous?'

'This is all very silly,' David Tower said. 'Stop it, the pair of you. Any minute now you'll say something you'll be sorry for.'

Jo seemed to take all her feelings into her hand like a bunch of reins and to pull on them hard to stop their galloping. She succeeded so well she was able to smile.

'If you really want to know, I'm looking forward to meeting Kojo *because* he's African. I don't know any Africans. It's time I did.'

This was stretching a point somewhat, and she wished her mother had not been listening. She was quoting Oliver because he had said something she should have thought of for herself. It took the wind out of Emily's sails, caused the parents to exchange a glance of relief, and made Roland raise his eyebrows in astonished admiration. As for Jo herself, she experienced what she told herself was the cool detachment of a poised woman of thirty or so; and she enjoyed it. There was a heady satisfaction in the judicious use of a generous withdrawal. And if that very fact somewhat diminished the generosity, at least it made for a general calm.

'You settle between you about meeting Kojo, then,' Deborah said. 'Your father and I will be coming too, of course.'

'We'll drive under our own steam,' said David, as fresh problems appeared—adults had no place in a Towering. 'We'll drive Kojo back, and Emily, naturally. You arrange all the rest as you like. How's that?'

It was fine, and Jo hastened to say so. She gave him a quick, loving smile because his 'How's that?' held no hint of mockery.

C

He had always treated her and Roland as reasonable beings. It was one of the moments when she thought with sympathy of Tamsin, coping with Uncle Robert and Aunt Helen, parents whose ideas of the family relationship were conventional to say the least. Of course one had to remember that Uncle Robert belonged to an older generation, that he was Great-uncle Robert —but that was no help to Tamsin, nor had it been to Camilla . . . Lucky Jo and Roland, Jo thought; and lucky Emily, she had no hesitation in adding, to have found her new home in this particular branch of the family.

A Tower Returns

CLIVE and Lydia collected Jo and Emily and Roland next day, as arranged. They then drove to the Evenses' and dropped Roland to wait with Oliver for Rose, who was to pick up Tamsin first. Robin was taking Sukey Miller and Martin Evens in the Spitfire; Hugh in the borrowed Hillman and Simon Evens and his sisters Penny and Rachel. Hugh was always very kind to the youngest members, who loved him for his lordly air and the feeling of being specially chosen for his favours.

The day was perfect—bright, crisp, with a high pale sky. The hard dry roads sang like magnetic tapes under the perfectly balanced wheels of the motorcade. For the young Towers the journey in itself was full of delights—merely to be driving, and driving all together, was enough to enchant these enthusiasts. Their talk was all of rpm and mph and mpg, of torque and pressures, heeling-and-toeing, twin carburettors, synchromesh and straight-through exhausts. After fifty miles they pulled up and changed drivers. Rose took the Spitfire, Clive the mini, Hugh the Morris, Robin the Hillman. Another fifty miles and the passengers shifted around. Jo and Oliver found themselves in the Spitfire, Rose still driving.

'You're the best driver,' Jo told her. 'The car even looks different when you're handling her.'

'It's just that the boys will show off. Robin's not so bad as Hugh —but he's not all that innocent.'

'Hugh's been driving the Hillman like a hearse,' Oliver said. 'But he's making the Morris shift. He's better than Clive.'

'Clive needs another car,' Rose said. 'He's like an old hen with the Morris. He's so afraid she'll drop to pieces he handles her like a clutch of eggs.'

Jo groaned. 'Oh roll on time! If I can't drive soon I'll die of longing. It'd be easier if I didn't know how.'

'I'll be ahead of you,' Oliver said, gloating. 'But it'll be years before I can get a car of my own. There may be some rich members of this family, but the poor ones outnumber them. Do you think Anthea could have made her fortune in America? Perhaps she's coming home with bags of gold. She might buy us all cars. Just as a nice cousinly gesture.'

'I must say I'm bursting to find out what she's been up to all this time,' Rose said. 'Any ideas, Jo?'

'Of course I haven't. Why should I have—suddenly—after all this time?'

In fact no one quite knew how Anthea had managed, though there were plenty of suggestions, some of them scandalous. The worst idea was that she had helped herself to some money from her father's desk. Or that she had wheedled herself into a job, answered an advertisement, say, for someone to look after children on the voyage. Or that she had charmed some handsome stranger into getting her across the Atlantic. How she had remained there so long, what her visa situation might be, how she had made herself a living—these were questions still to be asked.

'I wonder if we shall even like her?' Oliver said rather dreamily. 'You never know—she might be horrid. She might have grown a sneary-weary voice. She might despise us all—and make it plain to us.'

'She wouldn't be coming home if she felt like that,' Jo said firmly.

'Perhaps she's flying from the police,' suggested Oliver, rather hopefully.

'We haven't had any criminals in the family yet,' Rose said.

'And do we want them?' asked Jo.

This convulsed Rose, and Oliver and Jo caught the infection. They drove along making so much noise that a passing driver swerved at the sight and sound of them.

By this time Emily was with Tamsin and Lydia in Clive's Morris and Hugh was driving. Tamsin and Lydia talked and talked, but Hugh was silent, thinking perhaps about that girl in Austria; and Emily was silent because she had so much to think about.

Emily did not want to think about Anthea, she wanted to concentrate all her expectations on seeing Kojo again after nearly a year. But she took her position as High Tower very seriously. So her mind and imagination swerved giddily from Kojo to Anthea and back again to Kojo. How would he look now? How much would he have changed and what would that change tell her? He had been growing up fast and she could see from her own cousins that African boys were older for their years than English boys. She was frightened as well as excited at the thought of seeing him. She was accustomed now to being without her parents. She was one of the Towers. She had accepted the fact as they so fully had accepted and absorbed her. Yet somehow it all seemed too easy. How could she so soon have exchanged one way of life for another? Surely she was waiting for something more—but what? She was like some migrating bird, pausing for a while in one spot, and seeming almost ready to settle—yet all the time poised for flight further and further into the distant north or the warm south. Did any of them know—the cousins, young and old, who had gathered her into their counsels and handed her their affection? And if indeed there came a time when her continuing flight could no longer be delayed—would they ever understand?

Emily thought perhaps Oliver might know something of this— half because she liked him best of the boys and talked to him whenever she could, and half because he had a delicate and perceptive imagination. He was funny and made her laugh, he was full of nonsense, but it was like a transparent wrapping to his sympathy and understanding. Or perhaps the wrapping was transparent most of all to Emily because she herself had such a strange instinct for seeing clearly what was hidden.

However that might be, she would have chosen Oliver of them all to be her brother; but she had to beware, she knew, of trespassing on ground that was Jo's. For Jo, Oliver increasingly came first. In a way they all knew this, but without putting any sort of construction on it—without noticing, really, Emily thought, though more and more the two were found together. If you are with a thing all the time, how do you see it growing? How do you see a person growing, if it came to that? Emily had arrived in the Tower family fully fledged and with her eyes open, so in a way she saw them all a great deal more clearly than they saw themselves. She saw Jo and Oliver standing out from the rest; and somewhere in the confusion of her own particular gift for seeing too much, she was uneasy. . . .

By the time the young Towers reached the airport and got their four cars parked, Brian Miller had already arrived. When they all eventually converged, the nervousness of the father preparing to welcome back his prodigal daughter was painfully apparent. In fact Rachel, the youngest, asked in a piercing voice, 'Why is Daddy frightened?' Which at least had the advantage of breaking the tension.

So many Towers gathered in one place gave the impression of an organised outing.

'How are we going *exactly* to arrange the Towering?' Sukey asked. 'Do we brothers and sisters have a chance to say Hi first, or must we wait until the Towering welcome home thing's finished.'

'You must wait,' said High Tower, very firmly.

'Oh well—all right,' Sukey said reluctantly. She looked at the twins. 'What do you think?'

'This is a Towering affair,' Hugh replied.

'And what High Tower says, goes,' said Robin. 'If we Millers rush on ahead to greet our dear sister—the whole thing might as well pack up.'

'He's absolutely right,' Rose said. 'Where are the flowers, Tam?'

Tamsin shrieked. She had left them locked in the boot of the Morris. She and Robin and Roland went rushing off to fetch them, while the rest fretted and moaned at the inefficiency of Leaning Tower, who had after all undertaken to look after this part of the arrangements. The time was ticking over horridly by the time the three came pelting back.

'Heavens,' said Rose, as they approached. 'She's certainly done her stuff. How in the world shall we pay for all that?'

The bright gold of a mass of early daffodils seemed to shine across the field like a beacon. A good as a flare path, someone said.

'Oh Tam,' Jo cried, 'how absolutely super! How did you get hold of them? And *all* daffodils!'

'Much nicer than a mixture,' Lydia said.

'Better than anything!' 'Gorgeous!' 'Clever Tam!' they cried. And 'How much?' demanded Rose.

'Cheaper by the hundred,' Tamsin replied.

'And that's not cheap, I dare swear, ma'am. I vow you've spent a fortune ma'am,' said Oliver in his crabby-old-eighteenth-century-gentleman voice.

'I thought we'd have some each and sort of load her with them,' Tamsin explained, ignoring Oliver.

'She'll drop them and they'll all be broken,' Lydia objected. 'What do you think, Jo?'

'I think—oh I don't know. They'll be gorgeous anyhow.'

'Lay them at her feet,' said Emily dreamily, seeing the heap of gold and finding the picture very satisfactory.

'You want her to *tread* on them?' Lydia cried.

They stood together in the cold brilliant air outside the reception lounge, and saw Brian Miller waving furiously from the doorway.

'Coming in!' he shouted. 'The flight's just coming in!'

And indeed the big jet was already swooping in and drowning

his voice. They all stood gazing upwards as the plane dropped down through the faint gauze of mist still hanging in the upper air.

'Shut your mouth, Jo,' Oliver said. 'If anything drops off you'll swallow it.'

She laughed. The wind blowing across the tarmac frisked her hair back to front and into her eyes. She felt wildly excited, less by the arrival of the almost legendary Anthea than by the usual heady pleasure of finding so many of the family gathered into one place. She wanted to hug them all. She wanted, perhaps most of all, to hug the ridiculous Oliver—so instead she seized Rachel and twirled her round, and somehow that made them all start jumping about and waving their arms in excitement—even Hugh, even grown-up Hugh and Robin.

After that they grew cold waiting for Anthea to clear the customs and make her appearance. They began to stamp and grumble.

'There they are! There she is!'

'The Towering is in progress,' declared High Tower. They began to move forward towards Anthea and her father. 'Wait here.' And they all paused as ordered, standing there with their flowers, waiting.

The two figures came on.

'Taller than I remembered,' Hugh said.

'Yes. Taller,' agreed Robin.

'She looks very expensive,' Tamsin said. 'That coat!'

'Is it *mink*? I don't think we've had mink in the family before,' said Sukey. 'Do you think she'll—'

'—let me borrow it?' Jo finished for her.

'She must have made her fortune . . .'

'Married a millionaire . . .'

The strong wind across the airfield swung back the fur coat and flattened Anthea's dress. She put up both hands to grab at her fur hat.

For a second, the older members of the Towering faltered. There was a change in Anthea they had not anticipated and they felt flustered. As if she could read their thoughts as she approached them, Anthea snatched off her hat impatiently and tugged her coat round her.

'We did think she might be married,' Lydia said firmly.

It was the cue they needed. They rallied and surged forward, the daffodils bright in their hands, determined not to spoil the occasion, yet painfully conscious of Anthea's pale, rather wary expression, and of her father's obvious distress. He had his arm round her in a protective way that had already wiped out her years of wilful exile and neglect of them all.

'Here she is,' he said, releasing her and giving her a little shove towards her brothers and sisters and cousins.

'I'm your long-lost brother,' said Hugh, smiling and kissing her.

'He's Hugh,' said Robin. 'And I'm his twin. Remember?'

'There's a Towering to meet you,' Sukey said. 'I'm sister Sukey, Anthea—and these are the little ones. This is Penny. This is Rachel.'

They pressed the flowers upon her until her arms were full, murmuring their names, reminding her, claiming her for themselves whatever the circumstances might be.

'I'm Jo—and this is Lydia. We're still best friends ... Here's Oliver.'

'Tamsin. I was quite young when you left. Camilla's married—I expect you know about that. She's having a baby soon ...' Tamsin broke off and coloured bright red. Like you, she had almost said.

'Clive—'

'Simon—'

'—and Martin. Twins.'

'This is Emily, the one you've never met,' Rose said. 'And of course I'm Rose.'

'Of course,' said Anthea. The instant she spoke they remembered her. That slight drawl, the way she tilted up her chin. 'And these,' she was pulling the armful of flowers against her cheek, 'these are for me? How gorgeously Towersome.' She looked at them all, up and down and over, cautious, quizzical, as though she could read their thoughts. 'Thank you,' she said. 'What a welcome. I need it just now. I've just been telling my poor father about it.' She gave Brian Miller a quick, warm smile. 'He's distressed, poor dear.' Then she laughed. 'Don't worry, my darlings—everything is absolutely in order. I assure you I'm a married woman—married to Paul Darrell.' Then she paused and her face hardened. 'At least,' she said, 'I'm a widow. I've been a widow for a whole month now and I really must try to remember. Can you imagine? He was killed in Vietnam.'

Jo drove home with Clive, Lydia and Oliver. The Towering had not exactly broken up in disarray—on the whole they had all managed pretty well. Faced with tragedy they had rallied and behaved with dignity, listening in silence to Anthea's story, briefly, almost flippantly told.

Now Lydia sat crying sadly and quietly. 'It's so *awful*. How can she bear it? She's so young. Oh poor Anthea—poor, poor Anthea . . .'

'I suppose it's a good thing he was rich,' Oliver said. 'Still, if he was quarrelling with his family . . .'

'It sounds as though she's doing the quarrelling now,' Jo said. Distress as usual had made her angry. 'She had no business not to tell us. Turning up out of the blue like that—full of baby—making us think . . . Well I thought that was why she'd come running home.'

'It is why,' said Clive. 'You heard what she said. Honestly, if I were a rich man and I'd built up a huge concern, and then my only son tossed it all back in my face—I'd feel a bit sore.'

'That wasn't Anthea's fault.'

'But she said he met her at precisely the moment when the trouble with his family began. And then all that about taking up teaching . . . Look—I can remember thinking that Emily's father, Uncle Hugh, had been a bit of a traitor, going off to Africa like that instead of working in Tower Motors. But at least there were all the others—I suppose he wasn't really missed. But this chap—Paul Darrell . . . Damn it, he was their only son.'

'Oh don't, Clive,' Lydia said. 'What must they be feeling now? If he'd been a teacher from the start—perhaps he'd never have had to go to Vietnam.'

'Well, there you are—people often get the right ideas too late.'

'All the same, anybody ought to be pleased if their son married Anthea,' Jo insisted.

'Jo—not everybody loves a Tower, whatever you may like to think. I expect they wanted him to marry an American girl. Surely that's a pretty reasonable thing for American parents to want?'

Oliver shifted his shoulders uneasily. 'It's tricky. I'm not sure she should have bolted home like this. *I'm escaping*, she said. Perhaps she should have gone to the Darrells, as they asked her to. She's treated her own family pretty scurvily all these years. She might almost have been dead for all we heard of her.'

'She's here now,' Jo said. 'I'm mad with her and sorry for her, and sorry for the Darrells and mad with the Darrells—all at the same time. I suppose she'll stay here till the baby's born.'

'It'll be a British subject, if she does—won't it?' Oliver said. 'Treachery all round, if you ask me.'

'But they're all so unhappy—it's so miserable—so terribly sad!' cried Lydia, sobbing all over again. '*Poor* Anthea. *Poor* Darrells. Poor, poor Paul—we shall never know him now! Poor dears, poor dears,' cried sobbing Lydia.

'Oh Lydia, do stop it. It doesn't help any of us when you keep on wailing.'

'I do *hope* Jo hides a warm heart under that cold exterior,' Oliver murmured to Clive.

'Idiot.' Jo kicked out at Oliver's ankle, and he yelped. 'No softer than the toe of my favourite walking shoes,' she assured him. 'You seem to forget that there's still Kojo to come. Oh why did it all have to happen on the same day?'

'He'll be all right.'

'I've only just got used to Emily.'

'And how you've got used to her,' Lydia managed to say.

'Anyway, she's a cousin. And he's such a stranger, Oliver,' Jo said.

'Take it easy, girl. Emily loves him, and her father and mother must have loved his father and mother—or they wouldn't have made Mr Amponsah one of Emily's trustees.'

'We've got to like him—all of us. We've got to. If we don't we're beastly prejudiced racialists.'

'Keep calm,' Clive said. 'As Emily likes him so shall we, I daresay. Anyway, Jo, for Pete's sake—you don't love everybody who *isn't* black—why should you love everybody who is? It's just people. Some are nice and some are nasty.'

'It's the heart, lass, the heart that counts,' said Oliver, deep and rumbling and dramatic.

Clive grinned. 'Suppress him. And cheer up, you girls. Honestly —what a pair. Lydia's always crying for the woes of others, and Jo's always gritting her teeth over principles.'

'Is that what they are?' said Jo. 'How grand.'

She heard Oliver laughing comfortably and thought with annoyance how he must return to school in the coming week. Nowadays he got frequent weekends at home, but that did not mean that they always met. She was half angry with herself for missing him, half excited by his importance. The focus of her life was shifting, she was moving out of mere childish relationships. That meant that her friendship with Lydia, too, had deepened. It could have foundered on the rock of Emily's absorption into the family, of Jo's complete acceptance of her after that jealous start— but Lydia was generous and strong enough to defeat her own resentments. Thanks most of all to her, their friendship would last their lives now. They would share all their coming experiences, depend on one another, trust one another. Their children would play together on summer beaches too far away to be seen except as tiny pictures at the wrong end of a telescope . . .

Roland was home before Jo. After the others had driven away, the two of them set themselves the task of waiting in reasonable patience for the return of their parents with Emily and Kojo. They went to Roland's new room, where he was now most happily installed. It was over the garage and smelt, inevitably, slightly of petrol. In the old days when the garage was a stable the room would have smelt comfortably of horse. David had painted the walls and all the woodwork the same colour—a rather lurid yellow, Roland's choice, the accepted colour for old cars. The walls were stuck over with charts and posters of British and foreign motor cars, there was a car radio dismantled on the rickety table in the window, and a set of plugs so lovingly arranged in the lid of a box that they gave the impression of a very modern sculpture. Jo wished she had asked for the room herself.

'Tell you what,' she said. 'I'll give you the Bugatti.'

Roland had his back turned and for a second he did not move, only stiffened—with suspicious delight.

'You'll only be sorry and want it back,' he said.

'No, I shan't. Give a thing and take a thing . . . What a nasty boy. I was offering you a present. Probably changed my mind now.'

He turned at that. 'Jo. Please. I could stand it on the bookcase. Here.' And he went to the bookcase, which was cluttered along the top with manuals and handbooks of every conceivable brand of car, and he swept the lot grandly to the floor. 'Here, Jo.'

Looking at his eager face, she experienced the absolutely pure pleasure of giving pleasure.

'You go and fetch it, then,' she said. He was there and back in a couple of seconds, the little car cradled in his two hands. 'Now I've only got four hundred and ninety-nine,' Jo said. 'I must be mad.'

'You just go on being mad, then,' said Roland. He put the model lovingly in its place. 'I knew the room wasn't properly furnished,' he said. 'Thanks.' Then he lifted his head to listen. 'Ssh. Oh gosh—they're here.'

The car was just spitting over the gravel drive and up to the front door, the headlights sweeping a splendid arc across the face of the house. Jo was sure she had turned pale. She was cold with anticipation, terrified of falling short of this most difficult occasion. Her hands felt clammy and her ears buzzed as if she were running a temperature. And how much easier if she had been and could retire instantly to bed!

'Come on,' said Roland.

He grabbed her hand and tugged at her—and at once she saw that whatever else happened the stranger must not enter a house that seemed unwelcoming.

So the pair of them scrambled downstairs and Jo just managed to fling open the door before her father put out his hand to the latch.

The Stranger

EMILY's first sight of Kojo had hit her so hard that she thought she would have to lie down on the ground to prevent herself from falling there. He advanced towards her and with him came the first ten years of her life, the lovely African years when it had not occurred to her that she might ever have to live without her parents. Kojo's dark face, serious without being solemn, came out of the crowd of passengers with the steady increasing sharpness of a developing photograph. Yet he was different—how different— how much older. Then it was just as she had known it might be— for the first time it was entirely clear to her that what had been was truly gone for ever, just as the more boyish Kojo she had always known was gone, lost in this young man. She rushed to him, and he must have seen everything in her face, for he put down his luggage at once. He held out both hands, catching her by the wrists and steadying her as she stumbled.

'It is over now,' he said.

The shock, which she had waited almost a year to experience fully, seemed to patter in tiny light fragments through her mind. He was right. It was over. The old life was swallowed in the new; not forgotten, never forgotten, but absorbed.

'Are you well?' she asked formally, speaking in his own language

47

and delighting to do so again after so long. Then excitement swept out tragedy, and she took his hands and jigged up and down. 'Oh I'm so glad you're here! I'm so glad to see you! I've missed you all so much! How's Amma? Oh when shall I ever see her again? Will she ever come to England?'

'You will come back to Africa,' he said, with the smile she remembered.

'Oh yes! Yes—I shall!'

David and Deborah Tower, who had remained tactfully in the background while Emily greeted Kojo, now moved towards them. As light on her feet as she had been heavy, Emily danced between them and Kojo, making her introductions with pride on both sides.

'This is Kojo,' said Emily. 'Isn't it wonderful that he's got here at last? This is Aunt Deborah, Kojo—and this is Uncle David. He's a cousin, really, but the Towers call their *old* cousins Uncle and Aunt.'

'How are you, Kojo?' David said, holding out his hand. 'We're glad you've been able to come.'

'Emily's been so excited,' Deborah told him. 'I hope we can make you happy and comfortable. You're staying with us, of course.'

'Mrs Tower, that is very kind. Thank you.'

'Where else would you stay, except with me?' demanded Emily.

'Students live in hostels,' said Kojo. 'Very often. So it is most kind.'

'And now Aunt Deb will have a family of four to look after,' Emily said. 'There's Jo and Roland besides me and you.'

As she spoke she knew that a quick message had flown from David to his wife, and she knew it was a message of pleasure and satisfaction, because she had told them unwittingly how deeply she was settled with them. She remembered how she had arrived in the midst of this huge family, and how difficult it had been at first even to sort them all out. Now she was in the position of introducing Kojo. She was no longer the newcomer, the stranger—

there was a new stranger to take her place. Even though he was not a member of the family, he was to live among them for quite a long time. Emily felt herself to be his guardian. Perhaps she would have to fight for him—how many of them would like him, truly? If they were merely polite she would know it, and it would be difficult to deal civilly with them. It was not that she felt Kojo to be particularly noble or even amusing—but he was so kind and so clever; and he was Africa, he was everything she had lost of her early years—even her parents were somehow locked up in him and his sister Amma. But this was for her—not for everybody, not automatically for every other Tower. And in the town, too, at the works—what difficulties might confront him that she would long to shield him from?

She talked all the way home in the car, lapsing happily into the remembered tongue and being corrected in her manners by his replies in English—he was too courteous to exclude his host and hostess in this way. Then they were home, and as they came to the door Jo flung it open . . .

First, Jo saw Emily's face. She looked so happy it almost hurt—surely she had not been miserable all these months? Yet how much more life there appeared now in her face than any of them had ever seen. Second, Jo looked to her parents. They were smiling and easy. Then she managed to face Kojo Amponsah. He was not very tall. He had a mature and sensible face, a young man's face, not a boy's. He wore glasses, and he looked at her seriously, waiting for her greeting.

'Here's Jo,' her mother was saying. 'What a lot of introductions!'

'And this is Roland, Kojo,' Emily said, pleased with everyone and everything.

'Our names are alike,' Jo said. 'Hullo. Did you have a good journey?'

'Thank you. Very good. You are really Josephine?'

'Yes, I am. But I like to forget it. Doesn't suit me. I'm called Jo because of the one in *Little Women*,' she laughed. 'Sorry—I don't suppose you've heard about it. It's a book—'

D

'For girls,' he said smiling. 'My sister Amma has read it often. I am sorry I have not read it too.'

'You speak marvellous English,' Jo cried. 'Doesn't he, Mummy?'

'What would you expect me to speak?' asked Kojo, withdrawing a little behind his spectacles.

'I don't know, really. I suppose your own language.'

'But if I spoke my own language to you, Miss Josephine, you would not be able to reply. It is nice to be answered.'

Behind the glasses she saw that he was now laughing, but gently and courteously.

'Can I show him his room, Aunt Deb?' Emily was saying.

'Yes, you show him, Emily. And Roland can take up his luggage. I think you'll find everything you want, Kojo. Emily is so happy you are here. And so are we. We want you to be comfortable and to feel one of us.'

'Plenty of us to ask, if there's anything you want,' David Tower said. 'Later on I'll tell you all about the works. Or maybe Jo will. I believe she knows as much about it as I do.'

'Do you?' Kojo said to Jo, raising his eyebrows. 'But you are—'

'Don't say *only a girl*, or there'll be trouble,' said Roland. 'The girls in this family are thought to be as clever as the boys.'

'Or cleverer,' said Emily.

'Wait till he meets Rose,' Jo said, aware of polite surprise and possibly disapproval, and certainly doubt. 'My cousin Rose is at the College of Technology, too, Kojo. She is the cleverest of all. With motors, I mean—well, what else? She can take a car to pieces and put it together again—and it's not just as good, but better.'

'It's true, Kojo,' cried Emily. 'But do, *do* come and see your room.'

She pulled him to the stairs, and Roland picked up the suitcase and the hold-all. 'It's about time you turned up,' he said to Kojo, as they went up the stairs. 'Emily goes on and on about the Amponsahs. Besides, we don't know any Africans. Oliver says it's high time we had some African friends.'

'Who is he?'

'Oliver Evens. He's another cousin. He's clever, too. He's going to design engines.'

'He is older, then?'

'He's still at school. But he knows he'll do it.'

'This is a very clever family,' said Kojo, shaking his head.

'He isn't boasting, Kojo,' Emily said. 'Oliver really is clever. Also he's kind and funny. He's kind to me.'

'Then he is good,' decided Kojo.

Now Deborah Tower was coming up the stairs behind them. Roland threw open the bedroom door.

'Behold! The chamber of the guest!' he cried, in a Towering voice.

Kojo stood looking around him.

'Not very big,' Deborah was saying, as she straightened the towels by the wash basin. 'But you can manage all right, can't you?'

'It used to be my room,' Roland explained. 'But I've moved out.'

'For me?'

'Yes—I suppose so. But I like where I am now much better.'

Kojo looked at Roland, at Jo, at their mother. As he did so Jo knew with a dreadful feeling of guilt and anxiety that they were all overdoing it. They sounded so horribly nice. Surely he must hear it, the slight note of falsity and nervousness? Only Emily was justified in her affectionate reception of the guest; the rest of them were working much too hard.

'Would you like to unpack?' Emily asked, fussing round him. 'I'll help you.'

'I hope you'll be very comfortable and happy while you're here,' Deborah Tower said again, smiling. (*Oh Mummy, do pipe down*, Jo longed to cry.)

'Thank you, Mrs Tower. I shall like it very much here. I am glad to be with you.'

He sounded both confident and shy, and if indeed he suspected their warmth, he gave no sign. Yet how alone he must feel, Jo thought, standing in that strange place among unfamiliar faces that were not even the colour of his own.

Kojo was to have a week to settle in before starting work—that had been decided long ago. It was a sensible decision for he had a great deal to become accustomed to. He had not been out of Africa before, he had not been away very often even from his own home.

'Don't overwhelm him, Jo,' her father had said. 'You know what you are. You always want people to do everything at once. Let him find his feet a bit.'

'He can meet the others, surely?'

'Well, of course—but don't make it too big a dose, old girl. Let him off lightly.'

'You're being fussy,' she said. 'What d'you want to fuss about him for? He can manage.'

'I'll make the judgments on that, Jo.'

'You take such care of him I should think it might sicken him.'

'Let's stop talking about him, if you can't be reasonable. You're not very generous to newcomers, are you, Jo? You may remember you had some harsh things to say about Emily at the outset.'

This was unfair, and he knew it as well as she did, and tried at once to make amends. 'I'm being scratchy,' he said. 'It's all this business with C.M.H. and the take-over threat. We're all in a rather jumpy state. Still—I think I'm right about Kojo and the family.'

'All right.' It was not like Jo to find tears in her eyes—her upsets were usually angry ones and quite dry-eyed. 'When will he go to the works?'

'I'll take him round. I've arranged it with Gilbert. He can meet the other two trainees and get the smell of the place. I thought he might like to see over the Tech., too. Clive can look after that one.'

'What about Saturday morning?' Jo suggested. 'Emily and I can take him with us on Saturday morning. He'll like to see the old cars.'

'Yes. All right. You do that,' her father agreed. 'But don't forget what I said. Easy does it.'

Jo did not answer. *Easy does it* was the message she had wanted to give him . . .

The young Towers were so far thwarted in their dreams of setting up the Tower Motor Museum; that did not prevent them turning up at the works, Saturday after Saturday, to polish and clean and inspect their darlings, the vintage cars. There were always two or three of the cousins about, though fewer in term time, since various members were then away. Emily had very quickly become involved in this particular activity. She was an apt pupil and when presented with any problem she had an almost unnerving gift for going directly to the seat of the trouble, seeing the cause even if she was unable yet to contrive the cure. Jo and Roland were proud of her and convinced that she would become a good mechanic in time.

This new interest of Emily's obviously puzzled Kojo. He seemed unable to come to terms with the abilities of the Tower girls as they were related to him. He seemed, indeed, to be a little disapproving.

'I suppose he thinks a woman's place is in the home,' Jo said to Emily in private.

'I don't know if he does or not. His father might. Mr Amponsah's not a bit old-fashioned really. It's just that Africans have a lot of new ideas to get used to, and they've all come at once.' This was what she had heard her father say. Before Kojo's arrival she would not have been able to use the remembered words, and even now she could not speak her father's name. So the words rolled out as though they were her own, and she sounded alarmingly old.

On Saturday morning, Kojo went with Roland and the two girls to see the collection of old cars. The first person they met as they walked in through the main gate was Gilbert, the general foreman. He stopped when he saw them.

'One of you can come into the repair shop this morning, if you like.'

'Me,' said Jo—instantly ditching the stranger she had wanted so much to show around.

'Yes, all right; you,' Gilbert agreed. 'Okay, you others?' Emily and Roland nodded, Roland in a resigned fashion, Kojo looked bewildered, and Gilbert laughed in a friendly way. 'You'll get accustomed to the Towers in time,' he said—he and Kojo had met when David Tower took Kojo round the works in the middle of the week. 'How're you looking forward to joining us?'

For perhaps the first time since his arrival, Kojo broke into a wide, enthusiastic smile instead of his gentle, well-mannered one. 'I look forward very much. Very much indeed.'

'That's good. Ask for me when you arrive and I'll see you settled . . . Have you got overalls with you, Jo? Come on, then.'

Jo had not been in the repair shop for weeks and she was ready to hug Gilbert. Showing the old cars to Kojo was a minor delight compared with this one.

'Where's Tad?' she asked.

'His auntie's died. He's gone to the funeral.'

'Oh good,' said Jo. 'Sorry.'

Gilbert chuckled. 'I don't see why Tad Fletcher's auntie shouldn't do you a good turn—she wouldn't mind . . . Now look—this Austin. Dirty plugs you can clean. After you've done that, check over the usual—oil, water, battery, air. And see if you can work out the tangle the seat belts have got into. The car's in for washing, among other things. Do the inside for me, will you?'

'Okay. Shall I top up the oil if it's needed? What sort? Daddy's got a wondrous new window cleaner—a detergent thing . . .'

'I know. Glintex. We all got samples. There's one over on the bench if you want to try it. Leave the oil to one of the boys— sorry, I mean one of the workers—not boy as opposed to girl! You can top up the battery. You know where everything is.'

'Thanks.' Jo said. Maybe he'd feel bound to check over the lot when she had gone, but he would find he need not have bothered. She grinned at him and he grinned back. They had known one another a long time and they were beautifully easy together. These menial tasks were all he could allow her, but they were enough. They gave her the right to open the bonnet, hang over the engine, learn it lovingly . . . 'Has Tad got lots of aunties?' she asked.

'Now, then, my girl . . . Tad may be a worry to you youngsters, but he's good with the men. He's a stickler for the rules and I daresay he's quite right. I never should have let you lot into the works till you were older. How old were you, I'd like you to recall, when you first cleaned a plug in this shop?'

'I was eight,' said Jo. 'I thought you didn't like Tad?'

'Did I ever say so? I did not. I said he was keen for the union and that could mean trouble ahead. I thought he was a fanatic, see. He's not. He knows what he's doing, all right.' Then he gave a huge laugh and said to Jo behind his hand, 'I still don't like him.'

Somebody called him, then, and he went away. Jo was left in her corner, happily crooning over the dirty car. The day would come, she told herself complacently, when she would be consulted on the most delicate technical problems.

There was a good deal of noise in the repair shop, drilling and filing and bashing, the hiss of blow lamps and the general clatter of men moving about among machines, throwing wrenches and spanners down on the concrete floor, dragging metal tool-boxes and jacks from place to place. Someone was singing against a radio playing in the office. Across in the far corner from Jo two of the trainee boys were stripping down an engine; every so often Gilbert or another of the older men went to see how they were getting along. When they were alone the two lads, one short, one tall, talked all the time. Jo was too busy to listen to much of the conversation, though she was aware of an interest in birds and pop and a fabulous flow of colourful language that came mostly from the shorter boy. He left the delights of girls and records and started grousing about working conditions. That caught Jo's attention and she was immediately on the defensive.

'And now we've got to work with a ruddy nig,' said the smaller boy. 'Can you beat it? A nig in Milsom!'

'Someone to do the dirty jobs,' said the other. 'After all—muck on his hands won't show, will it?'

Jo straightened herself and stood swinging a large wet leather. As she emerged from the shelter of the car, the two lads became aware of her for the first time.

'Who're you talking about?' she demanded, startled by the ringing sound of her own loud voice.

One boy nudged the other, and the taller of the two said, 'What's that?'

'You heard me and I heard you,' Jo said. 'There's only one *nig* coming to work here that I can think of. He's my particular friend, Kojo Amponsah. He's staying at my home, actually.'

'And who're you, dear, when you're at home?'

'I'm Jo Tower, whether I'm at home or anywhere else.'

'Then make the most of it, I should,' said the taller boy. 'It might not last.'

Jo did what she knew she was bound to regret. She slung the leather. It caught the smaller boy hard across the right ear as he ducked. He yelped. The whole horrible picture of the possible consequences flooded into Jo's imagination in the split second that followed his cry: the delicate ear damaged for ever; a deafened trainee; everyone in court and huge damages to pay ... As the boy straightened up and she saw his face, she corrected all that to a flat, miserable conviction that she would never be allowed in the repair shop again.

'Well I never,' mocked the bigger boy. 'There's a naughty little cross girl for you.'

'You keep your hands off me, you dirty little so-and-so!' yelled the small one.

He went on to describe what he would do to her, and Jo fell easily into the same language.

'Shut your filthy trap,' was what she produced, more pleased than shocked with the unpleasant noise she made as she shouted it out. She might have controlled herself and retrieved some shreds of dignity if it had not been for the laughter of the older boy, clearly a more subtle type than his companion. 'As for you,' she told him, 'you look almost intelligent—so more's the pity you have to behave like a moron.'

'Wow,' said he. He picked up the leather and handed it to his companion. 'Here, Ron—give the lady back her property.'

Ron seized the leather and made a quick bound forward. Insisting that she would be an equal with the boys in all things, it had still not occurred to Jo that any one of them might consider her an equal when it came to combat. The promise of swift retaliation was in Ron's movement. If she was not careful she might find herself biting and scratching and rolling on the floor.

'Thanks,' she said—and grabbed the leather before he could do anything she would be unable to resist. At the same instant, she realised that the leather when it fell had gone straight into a pool of heavy oil. She felt the thick, oozy stuff almost bubbling through her grasping fingers.

In fact the two boys were in no better way, and they stood, the three of them, checked in their anger, their fingers dripping oil on to the floor and their overalls.

Happily, perhaps, Gilbert returned at this moment.

'What on earth have you all been up to?'

'Indoor games,' muttered Jo, turning back to the Austin and diving under the bonnet.

'Give me that leather, Jo. It's done for. Clean yourself up and get a fresh one out of the bin.' Gilbert looked suspiciously from one to the other. 'Chris—get a roll of clean cloth and wipe off that mess. Give the other two a length each. There's some grease on the shelf —get it off with that. Jo—do you hear? Clean up before you get at the inside of that car.'

'Yes, all right. Oh all *right*, Gilbert! It's not the first time I've had oil on my hands and I don't intend it to be the last.'

Gilbert gave her a final shrewd glance, then went about his own concerns. She snatched the cloth Chris offered her, got off the worst, and went on furiously brushing the inside of the Austin. She was grinding her teeth in rage and misery. What had been said about Kojo . . . What had been implied about the Towers . . . Neither bore thinking about—nor the fact that she had somehow made matters worse by behaving like a maniac. She felt gloomily that she had set a precedent—that one row could lead to another.

The boys returned to their job, Jo continued with hers. At first she imagined that her enemies were whispering together and laughing, but there was no sound but the sound of work. After a bit, Gilbert called Ron elsewhere, leaving Chris to finish off what the pair of them had started.

Presently Jo was aware that Chris had left his corner and was coming over to hers. She went on with what she was doing and he leant against the next car and watched her.

'Look,' he said at last, 'I know when to apologise. It was my fault, anyway. I egged him on. But you look rather good when you're angry.'

'Thanks,' said Jo—whether for the apology or the compliment she was not sure.

'I was the one who made the nasty remark about the Towers,' he reminded her, trying to catch her eye by shifting his position and bending down till he was on a level with her as she banged at the car's interior. 'Hey. Girl. I'm talking.'

Jo could not help looking at him, for by now he was practically hanging upside down in his attempts to gain her attention, and his hair, longish, was down over his eyes.

'You look like the greater hairy baboon,' she told him.

'I've got much nicer habits.'

In spite of herself, Jo laughed. They both straightened up and stood looking at one another, half suspicious, half friendly. Chris had a well-boned face that reminded Jo of Italian paintings—it was a face less of today than of always, a basic type that would lend itself to the costume of any age. He really did look too intelligent and generally well set-up to have behaved so boorishly, and it was clear that he laughed easily.

'Is one of your nice habits making satirical remarks about the Towers?' Jo demanded.

'I suppose I suit my conversation to my company. It's no good talking well-off to Ron—he wouldn't like it . . . Look—I've said I'm sorry.'

'The Towers made this place,' nagged Jo.

'And a fortune at the same time.'

'What if they did? Anyway, it isn't a fortune.'

'They made it by other men's sweat.'

'Do you honestly think they haven't sweated themselves? Why, there've only been about two of them in three generations who went elsewhere. It's been their whole life. And now it's our turn —and this time it's the girls as well—and it's being taken away.'

'Nonsense!'

'What else? What else, for goodness' sake?'

'You can work here just as much as I can.'

'Just as much! Thanks.'

'What do you want, then? To be called Miss Josephine and have us all pull our forelocks when you come in?'

'Of course not! Of course not!' Jo was beginning to shout almost as loudly as she had shouted at Ron. 'I just want it admitted —I want it owned up to—that William Tower made this place and I'm his great-granddaughter and I'm the works and the works is me. That's all.'

'And quite enough,' he said. 'But it could be I see what you mean.' He frowned at her, but half smiling, and shook his head. 'Look—don't you worry about that friend of yours. Ron's a bit of a trial, and lord knows he's not the only one. Even so—I'll look after your chum.'

She knew she could believe him. It seemed an oddly tranquil end to what had been a rather frightening episode. She mumbled some sort of thanks for this reassurance. Then there seemed nothing more to say. The morning was over, midday striking across the town. She took off her overalls and rolled them up, and then went slowly back to find Roland, Kojo and Emily. The Evens twins had turned up, and at once the small family collection cheered her and revived her normal aggressions.

'What'd happen to the old cars if Tower Motors was taken over?' Simon Evens asked.

'What should happen?' asked Jo sharply. 'They're not part of the works. They're a private collection belonging to Uncle Robert. You can't take away people's private possessions, you know.'

'Martin said they'd be sold, too,' Simon insisted.

'Martin doesn't know everything.'

'I know some things,' said Martin darkly. Jo was not his favourite cousin and he liked to argue with her. About a year ago, several people had complained that Jo was too bossy. Although no one had said this lately Martin still held the view that Jo was altogether too much inclined to order him and Simon about, whatever she might not do to other members of the family.

'Who's got the key?' Jo said, unaware of her young cousin's brooding. Emily handed it over and Jo locked up. The key was always handed in to the man at the gate as they left. This time, Jo decided to keep it. There were others, of course—holding one would not give her control over the shed where the old cars were collected. Still, it gave her a feeling of security to know that she could open the place at any time she thought necessary.

When they got home, David Tower was using the telephone in the hall. He sounded excited in a disagreeable way, and very irritable.

'The Board turned the offer down flat, Brian. Isn't that good enough to go on with?' Whatever the reply, it seemed to annoy him still further. He hung up almost without saying goodbye.

'Daddy—'

'Not now, Jo, please.' Then halfway to his little crowded study he paused and turned. 'Sorry. I'm in a mood. You want to know what's happened. The meeting was unanimous—they wouldn't look at such a poor offer. The take-over's off.'

'Well—aren't you pleased?'

'I wanted to be. Your uncle Brian Miller's a wet blanket ...
Though I suppose he only told me what I know—it's just that I
don't want to think about it. They'll make a bigger offer, of course.
We'll be swallowed. Sunk without trace in the great big sea of
County Mechanical Holdings.'

5

The Toppling

'I KNEW it would happen, the moment I saw your Uncle Saville, Jo,' Lydia said. 'He always seems to bring bad luck.'

'You can't blame him for what's happened.' Jo did wish the family had not the habit of saying always 'your Uncle Saville' as though he belonged to no one else at all, not even to his sister Deborah Tower.

'He sold out!'

'Don't be so dramatic about it. He only had a tiny little block of shares. Of course he sold out—he's always hard up. His shares couldn't make all that difference.'

'Why not? If you ask me they were the final straw and the whole thing's his fault.'

Jo did not reply to this. It was a ridiculous statement, false and ungenerous at the same time—unlike Lydia, who was usually prepared to give almost anyone the benefit of every doubt. Her unreasonable attitude was a measure of her distress, of the distress that had engulfed them all. For, as Brian Miller had gloomily said, a poor offer was bound to be followed by a better, and in the end by one too good for the shareholders to be denied. County Mechanical Holdings had acquired Tower Motors—to quote Uncle Saville, the Towers had toppled. Nothing remained but to consider which pieces, if any, could be picked out of the ruins.

It was a Sunday in early April. The whole business had dragged on till they were so sick of the strain that even the final disaster was a relief. It was in a desire for escape that Jo and Lydia, with Oliver and Tamsin, had got on their bicycles and ridden out to Thrumble Rows. It might have been a time for a Towering but they were all too subdued to make plans. It was a splendid evening at the end of a perfect spring day. This was the most magic time of the year at the Rows, with the beech trees spattered with vivid young leaf and the bluebells thick on the ground. All day there had been a wind to chase great clouds across the enormous sky. Now it was still, the sky had cleared entirely and the light was full and golden.

'What do you think will happen precisely?' Tamsin asked. 'I feel as if everything will change overnight. But of course it won't really.'

'You'll be all right, Tam,' Oliver said. 'Uncle Robert was going to retire anyway, wasn't he? You'll just go on living the way you've always lived. So will Uncle Peter and Auntie Jay, it can't bother the Cardew's much; they're so rich.'

Jo was sure he had not intended to sound bitter, but he did so, none the less. His father was Tower Motors' accountant, but his health was poor. Jo felt that Uncle John was almost sure to be prematurely retired and somehow that would seem to make Oliver head of his family—with an ailing father, a mother and two young brothers on his hands. The certainty of trouble ahead was already ageing Oliver, as Jo was quick to see.

Tamsin went very red at his tone. She did not want everything to be the same for her if it must be different for the rest. If there had to be a family disaster, at least she would share in it.

'It won't be any different for Lydia, either,' Jo said, aware of trouble on the way and hoping to head it off.

'No—the Holts can go on being poor as usual,' said Lydia cheerfully. 'But what about Clive? Will they keep him at the works?'

'He'll be all right,' said Oliver. 'After all his name isn't Tower. It's the Towers they'll want to get rid of first—and people like Dad who's had to go slow for nearly two years because of his illness.'

They sat together looking gloomy. Jo began to fidget. She was confused by her own emotions. She was so angry at the loss of the name *Tower Motors* that she was only starting to consider what the take-over must mean to the various members of the family.

'We ought to make plans of our own,' she said. 'I know they'll have to wait for years. But we ought to make them.'

'What sort of plans, Jo?'

'Well, we're almost all going to do the same sort of thing, aren't we? Not Lydia, I know—but Tamsin in a sort of way with her designing. There'll be a lot of us in a few years from now. Clive, of course—Hugh and Robin—Rose ... well, they're almost ready for work now. Then there'll be Oliver, and me a bit later—Sukey, perhaps—Roland certainly. And I expect the young twins, don't you, Oliver?'

'Not a doubt, I'd say. Martin's got all sorts of ideas, and Simon's not far behind him.' Oliver usually dismissed his young brothers, but today he was ready to give them their due.

'It's all perfectly obvious, then,' Jo said. 'We must start Tower Motors all over again.'

'Yes, of course,' said Oliver, as calmly as if she had suggested they should give a party. 'The pity is, we shan't be able to call it Tower Motors—something to do with trade registrations—I asked Dad about it.'

'But we'll do it, won't we, Oliver? We'll do it!' Jo cried, delighted that he had the same ideas as she had. 'We can call it Tower Enterprises or Tower Services, or something like that. If Great-grandfather William could start from scratch—then so can we.'

'There'll be an awful lot of difficulties,' Oliver said. 'For one thing we shall have bags of talent and no money to back it. Unless!!'

'Unless what?'

'There's just one rich young Tower—rich in her own right, I mean.'

'Emily.'

'Precisely.'

'She's got trustees.'

'She's also got a will of iron,' said Oliver. 'I'll bet you she can easily square her American aunt—and Kojo can go back and square his father—don't forget Mr Amponsah's the third trustee, but he's bound to be on Emily's side—he's known her longer than any of us. We might take Kojo into the firm, mightn't we?'

'But would he want to settle in England?'

'Rose,' said Tamsin, 'could persuade him.'

There was a second's startled silence, during which they looked at one another tentatively. Tamsin had put words to a matter no one had so far mentioned. Beautiful, frail, steel-handed Rose was increasingly seen at Kojo's side. She was older than he was, but he seemed far more the contemporary of the older boys, Clive, Hugh, Robin, than of Oliver; he was old above his years, responsible and steady.

'Yes,' said Jo. 'Well.'

And having come to a point at which they were all slightly out of their depth they were glad to change the subject . . .

All the same, it was something very much in all their minds, and Jo kept wondering if any of the grown-ups had noticed. The whole business was confusing. Conventionally, the argument ran that coloured boys pursued white girls—but anybody could see that Rose was the pursuer, while Kojo was tied in a knot by his own good manners. Jo did not know whether to be cross with Rose or to admire her independence of popular opinion. But mostly Jo was cross because she could not help feeling that Rose looked upon Kojo as a sort of gimmick—no one else had an African boy friend. It made her appear original and defiant. Delicate Rose dearly loved defiance.

When they left Thrumble Rows it was fast getting dark. Lydia cycled off home to Eason Elms in one direction, while Jo and Oliver and Tamsin took another way back to Milsom Parva.

'A good thing Uncle Brian got himself married before it all happened,' Tamsin said. 'Margaret might have felt he had enough to cope with, without landing himself with a new wife.'

'They'll keep him on,' Oliver said positively. 'He's so awfully good—he knows the territory inside out. But I don't think they'll put up with Uncle Peter Cardew for long. He's always been more decorative than anything else—I overheard Uncle Robert say that once. They'll certainly sack Dad. What about Uncle David, Jo?'

'They've given him a contract for five years.' Jo was not sure she was pleased. She had wanted him to make a proud gesture and tear the contract up. If he did so, he told her, he would never get another job in Milsom Parva—he might even never get another job. He was a young man, still—but these things could be tricky. He was a man with a family and pride would not feed them; one had to be practical. Besides, he had told her, he could not quite tolerate the thought of leaving the firm entirely in the hands of strangers. Whatever it cost them, some Towers and Tower relations must hang on. This was also the opinion of Hugh and Robin Miller. If their places were still there for them—and Uncle Robert had bargained hard before accepting defeat—then they would take what was offered, at any rate until they saw how things were turning out. Clive had said he could gain his experience elsewhere, even if the firm was prepared to keep him; and with this Oliver at present agreed. As for the girls—nothing had emerged yet of the attitude of C.M.H. to women engineers.

When Tamsin had said goodnight and taken her own turning for home, Jo and Oliver continued together. They were too burdened with their various troubles to talk at all for the first few minutes. They came to the Evenses' house first, but Oliver did not stop at his gate.

'I'll come home with you, Jo.'

'Let's look in at the Millers'. My mamma's been knitting tiny garments for Anthea's baby. She said if I saw her to find out what else she needs.'

'It'll be fun, really,' Oliver said. 'Won't it?'

'Do you mean the baby?' she asked, surprised.

'Yes. I do. Of course. There's Camilla's to be thought about, too.'

'Hers will be first by weeks ... Oh dear, it's all rather odd, isn't it?' said Jo. 'A starting-again thing. I don't know if I like babies or not. I haven't really known any. Lydia hasn't either—but she just *knows* they're gorgeous.' Jo laughed. 'She's just so soppy it isn't true!'

'You're not. Are you? Ever?'

She looked at him quickly, not sure whether he was mocking. But Oliver was not in anything like his usual mood.

'Do you mean I ought to be soppy?'

'You'll have to be, sooner or later. Won't you?'

'I don't know. Yes—perhaps. I suppose so. What about it?'

'I don't know whether I shall like you better or worse ... Oh well, I suppose I shall just put up with you, whichever way you turn out.'

'You make me sound like a pudding,' Jo said, because she was too pleased to say anything sensible.

'There you go.'

'Do you want me to swoon?'

He cheered up at that and began to sing in a throaty operatic tenor: '*Oh sweet maiden, When you're fadin' Away for love of one Whose dark eyeses, All surprises ...*'

'You've got blue eyes,' said Jo.

The moment she had said it she felt like casting herself into some dark cupboard and slamming the door. She could think of nothing to say, nothing to turn the remark into a joke. Indeed it was not a joke, the words had come easily for they fitted her thought—but that they should have been blurted out in such circumstances was too shaming to be endured.

After a pause that seemed endless, Oliver said, 'Yes, I have, haven't I? It's supposed to be my Norse blood.' His voice was not quite the voice she knew and he cleared his throat fiercely. 'Or hoarse blood, by the sound of it. Norse—horse—hoarse. Joke.'

'They might think we've come to cadge Sunday supper,' said Jo, flustered.

'Who?'

'The Millers, of course. We're on our way there—remember?'

'Yes, yes,' he said, 'I've got a good memory.' And he went along, pom-pomming under his breath and singing again *'Ah yes, Oh yes, Yes, yes, yes. Never shall forget the things I like to hear the best . . .'*

Then in a great burst of exhilaration, Jo shouted, 'Race you! Race you to the gate!'

And they went tearing off, Oliver a yard or two behind and crying 'Unfair! Unfair!' The wheels sang, the pedals made a fine whirring. Once the riders looked at one another through the near-dark and laughed, not certain why, not sure what the laugh admitted or denied . . .

'How lovely!' Margaret cried, when they appeared. No longer merely the dear charming person who had looked after Brian Miller's house and children, there was a subtle change in her manner. Now at last she welcomed visitors not only to his house but to her own. 'Stay to supper, will you? It's only cold meat and salad.'

'There—what did I say?' said Jo.

'Did you say there'd only be cold meat and salad?'

'No, Margaret, I didn't! I just said you'd think we'd timed it rather well.'

'And a good thing, too,' she said. 'Everyone's at home. The twins came for the day. They're going to sleep half a night and set out for Cambridge in the small hours.'

Hugh and Robin were home for the obvious purpose of sharing the family crisis—'And to bully me,' Anthea said. She had been besieged by distressed letters from Paul's family, urging her to return to America and make her home with them. She was treating them as ruthlessly as she had treated her own family when she cut adrift from them. 'I just don't want to think about them,' she had snapped once at Rose. 'They knew him much longer than I did. I suppose I'm jealous.' But after that one outburst she behaved as though Paul's death had wiped out the past years and nothing remained to her now but to concentrate calmly on getting the baby safely born. It seemed best to let her go her own way for the time being, though it was true that Hugh did try to talk to her about the business, even now.

'Did you get all those jackets and things from Mummy?' Jo asked Anthea.

'Yes, I did. I called her up just now to thank her.'

'She said I was to ask what else you want.'

'Everyone's marvellous. I've got a positive mountain of things.' Anthea's drawly voice was nicely spiced now by a faint American accent. She had a *parsitive* mountain; and it was highly unlikely that she would ever again *ring up* a friend—*call up* had become much more natural to her. 'Camilla's coming down on Tuesday— about her last chance as an un-mother. We're going to have a baby orgy together.' She laughed. 'Honestly, I hope I'm not short on maternal instinct, that's all. There's one hell of a lot to know about bringing up a litter. I keep reading books. They terrify me. I bet I get a problem child.' She looked at Jo. 'What about you? How's your maternal instinct?'

'Oh, I simply don't know, I don't think I've got one. Oliver has, though,' Jo said, as though that should be enough.

Anthea burst out laughing, but Oliver nodded solemnly.

'Jo's right. I shall dandle your little one—what's dandle, actually? It seems to be something you only do to babies ... Anyway, I shall do this dandling business with great skill. You'll see. And if you like I'll sometimes bath it and put it to bed for you.'

'Oliver—you won't know how.'

'My maternal instinct will triumph,' Oliver said, smoothing an imaginary apron, and folding his arms in a comfortable, nanny-like way on his stomach. 'Now, Peregrine, we'll have no more of that splashing, if you please. Once again, and it's into bed with no milk or biscuits.'

'Shall I really call him Peregrine?' Anthea wondered.

'Why not? It means pilgrim, doesn't it? He could be a pilgrim son instead of a pilgrim father.'

'Oliver, you're the dottiest of all the family!' cried Anthea. 'Still a pilgrim son is rather a poetic idea, I think.'

'He might be a pilgrim daughter,' Jo said, speaking up as usual for her own sex.

'Oh if he's a daughter, I've decided on a name.' Anthea looked at her hands. 'I think the first girl of a new generation should be called after her grandmother.'

'Yes,' said her father, rather too quickly, perhaps, but he thought this might be a sign of conciliation in Anthea. 'What's Mrs Darrell's name?'

'I haven't a clue. I was thinking of my mother, not his. Patricia Mary. I could call her by either.'

'Yes. Yes, you could, certainly.'

'Well, I'll have Patricia and leave Mary. If it's a daughter she'll be Patricia Margaret,' said Anthea, without giving her step-mother so much as a glance.

It was Jo who looked at Margaret. But Margaret had already turned quickly to Brian, with a smile so content and so private that Jo instantly looked away.

Emily was the one who was most irritated by remarks in the town on the take-over by County Mechanical Holdings. She had become almost aggressively a Tower during the last few months. It infuriated her to hear such opinions as 'About time, too'; and 'Time their high and mightynesses were taken down a peg'. She was filled with a hot anger none of the others had seen before. She stamped about the house, pale and glowering and mouthing mysterious threats that sounded all the worse because she used Kojo's language instead of her own.

'Don't Emily!' Roland cried. 'Strange words are terrible. Don't

do it!' He appealed to Kojo, who was listening and smiling. 'Tell
her not to. I'm sure she's doing awful curses. If you make a curse
in a strange language—it happens.' Roland was not sure if he had
actually been told this, or whether it was an idea of his own; but
it sounded reasonable. 'If only you'd thought of it sooner,' he said,
'you might actually have cursed away the take-over. You must
have known it was going to happen. It's the sort of thing you do
know about.'

'No, it isn't,' Emily said quickly. 'I've stopped all that, actually.
Kojo says I've grown out of it.'

This 'Kojo says' business was becoming a shade tedious to some
of the young Towers. Emily made him sound a dreadful know-all.
If he really said half the things she claimed, he was making a lot of
critical comments on the Tower family, on the works, on Milsom
Parva and on England generally that were irritating if not actually
offensive. Jo did not necessarily believe this to be so. She knew
how anxious Emily was to present Kojo as a kind of super-person,
and to do so she might very easily interpret his remarks rather
freely—for he had never been heard to say these things himself.

When Emily first came to live with them, Jo had protested that
they would all spoil her with their care, with their desire to make
up to her for what she had lost. This in fact had not happened, for
Emily had retained her essential aloofness. But what might have
happened to her seemed very likely to be happening to Kojo.
His self-confidence blossomed and increased as they drew him ever
closer into their counsels—so desperately anxious to treat him fairly,
to make him entirely at home, that they were all set to turn his
head. It was certainly not Kojo's fault that when he behaved as
they encouraged him to behave they felt, though secretly, that he
went too far. For however hard they tried, these kind and intelligent Towers, they were still fighting what they believed themselves
to have defeated—the sad old prejudice that a white skin was somehow a better thing to have than a black.

With one thing and another, the confusion among the Towers
through that fine April weather and into May, was very great

indeed. It was somehow inevitable, as though in celebration of the end of an era, that Aunt Harriet should die suddenly, with no warning at all, as she was walking in her own garden with Aunt Silly Milly and her companion Miss Surplice. Poor old Aunt Harriet! There was too much going on for her funeral to be much of an event. The immediate result was the retirement of Aunt Silly Milly to a nursing-home, for the shock had been great; old Uncle Thomas Tower had moved in there six months ago—which left only Uncle Robert to represent the oldest generation. In the curious fashion of time and life and fate, the family balance was partly redressed a few days later: Camilla gave birth to a son.

'Now I can't be godmother,' mourned Emily. 'Boys never have two, do they? Tamsin'll have to be it. Oh what a bore!'

'We must send a telegram,' Jo decided.

'With all our names—our Towering names, Jo. Let's write it out.'

'It'll cost rather a lot. Had we better wait and be sure the others will pay their whack?'

'*No!*' cried Emily. And for the first time ever, she said, 'I've got plenty of money. I'll pay if you like.'

It was nine o'clock on a Saturday morning, and the news made them forget even the usual spell at the works. Aunt Helen had telephoned from London, where she had gone to be with Camilla until the baby was born. She had telephoned every Tower household in strict order of precedence, which was lucky for the David Towers—since David was the only surviving male Tower in the third generation he got the news immediately after Uncle Robert, the baby's grandfather.

'I'll ring Lydia,' Jo said. 'She sometimes thinks of good messages —greetings, I mean. You know the sort of thing.' What she really meant was that she could not possibly resist speaking to Lydia at such a moment. She rushed to the telephone and Lydia, as though by instinct, rushed at her end to snatch up the receiver.

'Is it you, Jo? Isn't it fabulous! Isn't it terrific! Oh isn't she *clever!*'

'Yes, I suppose so,' Jo answered.

'I can't wait to see him!' Lydia cried.

'Oh I can,' said Jo. 'I don't want to see him till his wrinkles have got a bit ironed out.' She would have had to admit that she had frequently averted her gaze from little wizened things in prams outside shops in the town, but she was prepared to endure them in a slightly larger, smoother size.

Emily was fidgeting at Jo's elbow.

'Tell her about the telegram!'

'Emily wants to send Camilla a Towering telegram,' Jo told Lydia. 'You're good at greetings. What shall we put? All our Towering names, of course—but what message?'

'Something calling him New Tower . . . ?'

'Oh lor'—must we?' Jo sounded revolted, as indeed she was.

'What's wrong with that?'

'Saccharine . . . Let's just put Towering Good Wishes, and then our names.'

'You asked me,' said Lydia, pained. 'That sounds plain hearty to me.'

'Well, good wishes are always hearty, aren't they?'

'Oh all right,' Lydia sighed. Then she said, 'Clive's just come in. Shall I ask him if he'll pay his share?'

'Yes, and ask him what we should say.'

In the end, it was Roland who said they should put *Love and good wishes to Camilla and Son*; and then sign all their names. Too late they realised they should have included Alan in the greeting. He was no Tower, but he was after all the baby's father.

As Jo and Emily left the post office and turned for home, they saw Kojo ahead of them. He went to the works on alternate Saturdays, and he should have been there now. The routine had been going on for a good many weeks, so what had changed it?

Emily stood absolutely still for a second. Then she said in a low, trembling voice—'His face! His poor face!'

His back was turned, she could not see his face, but she knew none the less. Jo felt herself chill and shiver, for she had accepted that Emily was no longer inclined to see things not yet encountered.

In a wild desire to prevent some unimaginable scene in the street, Jo grabbed Emily and hung on to her. They were not far from home. Kojo must get to family territory before they knew—before they saw his face.

Emily realised this as clearly as Jo did, and she made no attempt to pull away and rush after him. They stood tensely together until he was out of sight, then followed fairly fast. He was fumbling at the door handle before they caught up with him. He was almost safe, Jo said to herself. In a panic of anticipation, she found herself wishing that he need never turn, that she need not know what had happened. But he heard them behind him, and he did turn.

Towers in Trouble

'LEAVE me—leave me . . .' Kojo said. And he pushed into the house ahead of the girls, thrusting away Emily who had seized his arm. 'I am all right. Leave me. I will go and wash. It is nothing.'

It was not the fact that his clothes were dusty and even torn, nor the blood on his face—not much of it, but enough. It was the absolute misery of his expression, in which humiliation was mixed with fear and disappointment and a terrible bitter sorrow.

There was no one else at home. Roland had gone to the works and the parents were both out. The two girls watched Kojo stumble his way upstairs.

'Where are your glasses?' Emily called after him.

He put his hand on his pocket, but did not turn. 'I have them. Broken. Please do not worry, Emily. I have an old pair to use if necessary.' Then he was up the stairs and into his own room. The door slammed behind him.

'What shall we do?' Jo said in a shaking voice. 'Someone's beaten him up! We should have listened to Chris! We must help Kojo, Emily! We must help him! Oh I wish Daddy was here. . . . I wish Oliver was here . . .'

As she spoke, there was the sound of a car driven fast and

furiously. The door burst open and Rose and Roland rushed into the hall.

'Where is he?' Rose demanded. She was wearing overalls. Her hands were black. 'They got as good as they gave, anyway,' she said. 'I happened to pick up a tin of cylinder black. It doesn't come off as easily as blood.'

Jo could only think that Rose, sounding wildly dramatic and flaming with anger, looked wonderful. She was like a coiled wire, humming with tension, and looking smaller, neater, but more deadly than ever before.

'She knocked them down, both of them,' Roland said, his voice squeaky with fright. 'She did, Jo. It was Ron was the worst—then that chap Williams from the paint shop. They went sort of mad. They went at him. They banged him about. He'd have managed if he hadn't broken his specs—but he simply couldn't see.'

'Where was Chris?' Jo demanded. He had promised to look after Kojo and he had failed her.

'They'd locked him in the loo,' said Roland.

'Gilbert, then . . . Oh—not on duty this week.' Jo stamped with fury. 'They planned it for when he wasn't there!'

By this time Rose was in the kitchen filling a bowl with hot water and looking for disinfectant.

'Don't mind if I help myself, do you, Jo? Emily—go and ask Kojo whether he'll come down or whether he'd rather I went up to him.'

Emily scuttled off and they heard her knocking at Kojo's door and calling, calling. After a bit she triumphed and he opened the door. She spoke to him in his own language and somehow she persuaded him to come down—no one else could have done— even Rose knew that. Just for a second, as he came into the kitchen where the others waited, Kojo looked no more than a pathetic boy. Then he braced himself. He sat down without a word on the stool Roland had placed for him by the sink. Rose went to work on his face.

It took some time, for Kojo had been sent flying and his face had scraped along the gritty floor which was not improved by the addition of broken spectacle lenses. Rose pulled out small glass splinters with eyebrow tweezers. She was clever and patient and gentle. Neither she nor Kojo spoke and he never once looked at her. But Jo and Emily and Roland could not stop talking.

'Wait till Daddy gets in!' Jo cried. 'Wait till he hears, that's all. He's still in charge of personnel—he's the one who'll have to cope. And I wish it could be me!'

'That's done it,' Rose said at last, throwing down the sponge she had been using, and patting at Kojo's sore face with a pad of tissue. 'How is it, Kojo? How does it feel? Is it dreadfully sore?'

Her voice was achingly soft, but he did not answer. He got up at once and went out of the kitchen and upstairs to his room again. Rose watched him go in silence, wiping her hands as she did so. 'A word of thanks might help,' she said, in a thin cold voice.

'You don't understand—' began Emily.

'No, no—of course not!' Rose cried. 'Only Emily ever understands. Only Emily knows anything at all about Kojo Amponsah . . .'

'Well—' began Emily.

'Oh be quiet and let me get out of here!' snapped Rose.

She pushed Emily roughly on one side and stormed out of the kitchen. The door slammed so violently behind her that the house shook. The car door was wrenched open, hurled to, and the car cracked into gear and was away.

'People shouldn't drive in a temper,' Roland said. 'Suppose she had a smash . . . ?'

Emily went out of the room as though everything had become too much for her, and Jo was able to ask Roland what Kojo had done to spark off the incident of the paint.

'Nothing. Absolutely nothing. He did nothing, Jo.'

'Well, then—how did it start?'

'He and Ron were on the same engine, and Williams came in with this can of white paint. Ron said, "What's this for?" And

Williams said he'd been told to start painting the walls. Ron said, "Only the walls?" And Kojo said, "Do you want him to make a white floor, then?" And he laughed. And Ron said, "Truth is, mate, we'd like everything white." First they were just giggling and silly. Then Kojo went to get a spanner off the bench and Williams tripped him. He went down flat and his glasses broke. So it started—like I told you.'

'But Chris? You said Chris was locked in the Gents . . .'

'He was. He was banging and shouting.'

'So they must have planned it. Got him out of the way first . . . Go on.'

'Well, then,' said Roland, 'Rose came in.' He let out a great whistling breath and his eyebrows rose almost to his hair line. 'It was like a sort of whirlwind. Honestly. I don't know how she did it—it was like judo or something. Suddenly there was Williams on the floor. And there was this open tin of cylinder black on the bench. So she picked it up. She kept shouting to Kojo to go, and at last he did. But I stayed.'

'Then?'

'Rose put her hand into the black paint and it came out all gooey and dripping. She slapped Ron's face twice, first one cheek and then the other. You should have *seen* it. He stood there and let her do it. You'd think he was hypnotised.'

Remembering her own trouble with the oily leather, Jo could appreciate this. But Roland's description of the incident had left her feeling shaken almost to the point of trembling. Such things did not happen singly, even she knew that. This was only the beginning of trouble.

The row that followed the matter of Kojo and the trouble at the works echoed and reverberated through the family, through the works, through the town. Everyone knew about it. There were sharp divisions of opinion. Some said such a thing could never have happened if the Towers had still been in full control. Others considered it was time the Towers took a beating, and that it was they who suffered through Kojo, their protégé. David Tower found it one of the most worrying things that had happened since he was made responsible for works personnel. He felt that it threatened his position in the firm, since he was now answerable to big business of a kind he knew to be ruthless. He was the one who had introduced Kojo into the works—the matter was entirely concerned with his household, his affairs. For the first time racial prejudice stirred in Milsom Parva, and it was he who had given it a chance to appear. He spoke, even, of offering his resignation. It was Uncle Robert, no longer spoken of as the Duke of Milsom Parva, who urged him to ride the storm and refrain from heroics.

'Don't give them a chance to get rid of more of us,' he said. 'It's essential that there should be a Tower influence still.' This went round the family and stiffened them at a moment when their spirit was very low.

Kojo himself had remained cool, though if anything more reserved than hitherto. He had reported for work as usual on the Monday morning after the incident. By that time Gilbert, alerted at his home on the Sunday, was dealing with Ron and Williams.

'I'd have liked to sack them both,' he told Jo, next time they met. 'But you know what that would mean. Tad Fletcher would have had the rest of them out on strike before I could turn round.'

When Kojo got home from the works that Monday evening, Deborah Tower was looking out for him.

'How was it?' she asked anxiously. 'How did you get on?'

'Oh very well, thank you, Mrs Tower. I work and I do not speak. Much easier.' He smiled at her troubled expression. 'Others must put up with this all the time. I have not so much to complain about, have I?' Then he said, 'I am learning fast. More than just mechanics.'

'It is not the right sort of *more*,' sighed Deborah. 'Here are your spectacles, Kojo. They did a rush job on them.' And she was glad of a chance to change the subject.

This was only two days after the incident. It was in the weeks that followed that the controversy mounted, the town divided and the strain increased.

'Why did it have to happen exactly now?' Jo grumbled to Lydia. 'We all want to hang on to everything we can and this makes it much more difficult. I'm sure people look at me quite differently now that Tower Motors has been swallowed up. And some of them more differently still because of Kojo. Oh I do wish he'd never come here—and I hate myself for wishing it.'

'It's stopped him being so stuck on himself,' said Lydia, very shrewdly for her. 'Poor Kojo. I think he's having a beastly time. I wonder he doesn't just pack up and go home.'

'And another thing,' Jo said gloomily, 'Emily's Aunt Sam has written again. She wants her to go to America for all the summer holidays.'

Emily's unknown American aunt, her dead mother's stepsister, was a Mrs Sambrook. It was Oliver who had called her Aunt Sam, and the name had stuck. Since she was the third trustee under Humfrey Tower's will, along with Mr Amponsah and David Tower, it was only reasonable that she should want to meet Emily.

'Daddy's your proper guardian,' Jo had said rather fiercely to Emily. 'So if you go off visiting—you'd better not forget this is your real home.'

The idea of losing Emily at this point was not at all congenial to Jo. Kojo was Emily's responsibility initially, but if she went away the David Towers must look after him. This would not be easy.

The rest of the young Towers, who had none of Jo's private reservations in the matter, had rallied instantly to Kojo's support after the ugly business at the works. It had given him enormous importance in their eyes. He seemed to represent a triple challenge —the challenge against reaction in the face of progress, of the young against the old, of the Towers versus too large a proportion of Milsom Parva. Rose stalked around the town knowing herself talked about, blatantly inviting the frowns of motherly women who had admired her looks in the past. Their lips tightened now as they recalled the tale of her striking down Williams, daubing Ron—such appallingly unfeminine behaviour. Only a few months ago she would have got away with it, she would still have been admired—they would have accepted even her bold friendship with Kojo. But as Oliver had said, the Tower mystique was like an old alarm clock—when the hour came for the bell to ring it gave out nothing but a wheeze and a tinkle . . .

For all this support and sympathy lavished on Kojo, only Emily understood what the incident had really meant to him. The beastliness, the enmity, the cruelty—he could endure all these with unshaken dignity. What utterly debased and humiliated him was Rose's part in the affair. Unable to defend himself, the blood dripping from his face, his glasses broken, the two lads holding him down, he had had to suffer the indignity of being defended by a woman.

'He'll never forgive her, Jo,' was what Emily said.

'They're still friends. He hasn't changed.'

'She may not notice it yet, but she will. It wouldn't be possible for him to forgive her,' Emily insisted. 'How could he?'

'She saved him.'

'That's just it. Surely you can see that he'd rather have been tarred and feathered than owe his escape to Rose.'

'Do you mean just because she's a girl?' Jo asked in a disgusted voice.

'You wouldn't understand, Jo—how could you? And she wouldn't, either. But I understand. I truly mean it when I say he'll never forgive her. Never. Never.'

'Somebody's mad,' Jo said helplessly.

So when Tamsin said that she, too, had an African friend, a fellow student just concluding a course at the Art School, Jo groaned and prophesied more trouble ahead.

'Not a boy—a girl,' Tamsin said. 'I honestly think my poor mamma would die if I turned up with a dark boy friend. She's got such Anglo-Saxon ideas. No—Adwoa's from Ghana, too.

She'll be going back there soon. She and Kojo ought to get on together.'

'Could it be as easy as that?' Jo wondered. 'Suppose you were expected to get on with every other English girl? Oh Tam, I do wish you'd leave her to find other friends. Kojo's probably a member of a tribe that hates hers, or something of that sort. There'll be terrible trouble—you see if there isn't.'

The depths and subtleties of this business were beginning to declare themselves to Jo. It was not enough, she saw suddenly and painfully, to be more broadminded than the neighbours, and vain of being so. What had she expected? What had she imagined they would do for Kojo? Probably she had seen him happily absorbed into their society, becoming one of them. *Quite one of us; almost one of the family*—these condescending catchphrases would not do. To become one of them was the last thing Kojo would—or should —desire. Both sides, Jo thought, fumbling about in a mind dim with difficulties, needed to re-make themselves. The idea was too obvious yet too enormous to digest. It meant a whole new world. Yet Jo knew that she could not set this huge idea aside and pretend to forget it. However vaguely, she had become aware of an outline, like a map without rivers or towns or mountain ranges; she could not retreat from it. She must, indeed, make her own contribution, however modest, to the vast whole, by trying to understand and accept that Kojo's manhood had been damaged by Rose's defence—and she must not blame him if, as Emily claimed, he never forgave Rose.

It always came back to Emily—so much had happened that could not have happened if she had never come to live in Milsom Parva. The effects of her arrival still bounded and re-bounded like an echo, or like an image seen in a hall of mirrors. What Jo envied Emily, as she herself struggled to understand the problem of Kojo, was her time in Africa, her growing years when she had had the fortune to be among people of different races who were civilised enough to see one another whole, not in fragments of colour or feature. Jo wished with all her heart that she had known

Emily's father, Humfrey Tower, and her American mother. Between them they had made a girl whose mind was quite clear about people.

In spite of Jo's gloomy prophecies, Tamsin brought home her friend Adwoa Paku and everyone who met her liked her. Adwoa was better placed than Kojo, for she had been in England some time and had found her way around. The Towers, too, had had the ice broken for them by Kojo's arrival, and they were much more at ease with Adwoa in consequence. She was easier to get on with, anyway, for she was gay in manner, where Kojo was serious, and had soon discovered what the English liked to laugh at. She was a small girl, neat, graceful and intelligent. She had trained as a nurse at the hospital in Barhampton and was now doing a short course on dress design at the Art School. At the end of the summer she would return to Ghana. She had plenty of friends and shared a flat on the coast at Milsom Magnificorum with three other girls, one Ghanaian and two English. Rather surprisingly, in Jo's view, Aunt Helen took to Adwoa and invited her to stay. She and Emily, too, found a lot to talk about. The difference in their ages, as was usual with Emily, made no difference whatever to their ease with one another.

'She said Kojo must relax,' Emily reported to Jo.

'How do you know?' Jo felt somehow outraged—Emily always knew such a lot.

'He told me, of course.'

'Does he tell you everything? You sound like somebody's mother. There's a boy at Oliver's school whose mother says, "Peter tells me everything." Oliver says she'd swoon clean away if he did.'

'If everything is what Kojo wants to tell me—then he tells me. That doesn't mean always.'

'Nobody tells me everything,' Jo said crossly. Then she added, half to herself, 'Oliver might.'

'What do you mean—he *might*?'

'If we got married or anything,' Jo said, losing her breath as she heard herself saying to Emily what she had never mentioned to Lydia. Since her last birthday things that had seemed away in another age had suddenly appeared quite close at hand.

Emily said, 'But you're cousins.' Which was what Lydia would say, Jo realised, and probably why they had never spoken of the matter.

'Cousins can marry.' Jo had recently made sure of this in a roundabout fashion, from Uncle Saville. He must have known exactly why she was asking, but he had been decent about it and given no sign.

'They're allowed to,' Emily agreed. 'But it's supposed to be a bad thing.'

'*What* a lot you know!' cried Jo, in a snappish voice. 'In-breeding, I suppose. Lydia's always talking about in-breeding— only it's dogs and horses with her.'

'Well, there you are. If you breed animals wrongly they come out the wrong shape.'

'Oh, so you think that's what would happen to my children— six toes or four ears, or something. I'm not all that keen on being bothered with a family, anyway.'

'Aren't you? What about the Towers? You can't be the one to stop the tower growing, can you?'

'The others can look after all that.'

'Well, anyway,' began Emily. But there she stopped.

'Yes? Go on.'

'Nothing. I've forgotten what I was going to say.' Emily bent forward and her hair swung to hide her face. She had not forgotten what she had been going to say, and Jo knew she had not forgotten. She was beginning to know the signs of Emily's pre-knowledge, whether or not it finally came to a head. Emily had most certainly been going to say, Well: anyway, there was no likelihood of Jo and Oliver marrying.

'This is a stupid conversation,' Jo said, a little shrill. 'Stupid! Stupid!'

'Don't be cross!' Emily cried. 'I don't know how it started, anyway, and I don't really know what I'm talking about.' She shook back her hair. 'He's the nicest, Jo—the best of the boys, isn't he? He's my favourite cousin except for this house. When I first came to England—my very first night, when I was at Aunt Lucy's and we were both so miserable and everything seemed awful—he made me laugh.'

'Yes—he's gorgeously funny sometimes,' Jo said. She heard the fondness in her voice and felt frightened out of her wits by it. Again she had the feeling that life had taken a huge leap forward without her realising what was happening. 'Emily—you're a dreadful girl. I believe Kojo does tell you everything. I expect he can't help it. It sounds as if I can't, either.'

Emily laughed and the tension eased. They began to talk rather quickly about other things—about the christening of Camilla's son, James, and about how soon, now, Anthea's baby would be born—even whether she would marry again, whether she would recover from her tragedy and be happy with another man—as her father had found his second happiness with Margaret.

All this was much pleasanter than thinking about the take-over of Tower Motors, and better than wondering if they would be prevented from working about the place on Saturday mornings. And it was much better than getting fussed about the veteran car collection. The chief trouble about that was that no one seemed able to tell them what was happening. Jo kept nagging her father to tell her the position, but he was too bothered about things in general to pay the attention she felt the matter required.

'The cars belong to Uncle Robert, don't they?' she urged.

'Yes—I suppose so. Quite honestly I don't know what the situation is.'

'Can't somebody do something to find out?' Jo cried, frantic at the idea of the collection passing through sheer inertia into alien hands.

'Jo, don't keep on and on like this. I've got enough on my plate as it is—surely you can see that?'

'It's important.'

'I know—I know. It's just that it's an outside interest at the moment. We'll come to it later. I must admit,' he added, giving her some attention at last, 'that I can't help feeling the collection is part of the works. If so, it's bound to change hands with all the rest.'

For a moment Jo was quite speechless. Then she pulled out the one practical possibility she could see among all the emotional arguments she had in mind. 'It must be worth an awful lot of money.'

'That's just it. It is. Someone will have thought of that.'

'I told the others it was a private collection—as private as mine upstairs. I said nothing could possibly happen to it.' As she spoke she remembered that she had the key of the shed in her possession still. Her mind immediately seethed with wild possibilities— locking themselves in and standing a siege—driving the cars away at dead of night—even setting fire to the collection rather than lose it to strangers. 'I'll have to go and ask Uncle Robert,' she said. It was a big decision, for she never approached Uncle Robert with ease or pleasure.

'Yes—do that,' her father said.

She looked at him quickly, for he sounded weary beyond words. It was difficult for her to see his face objectively; she knew him too well to have any clear idea of his features—she could hardly have described him to a stranger. Now she suddenly saw change in him. He had always been easy, almost gay in his manner among them. Now something wary had crept into his expression and his mouth had tightened. He looked like a man who knows bad news is coming and has braced himself to meet it. She thought of Uncle John, Oliver's father, how he was so often ill, so that there was a cloud of anxiety very often over that household. Anyone could suddenly become ill, Jo realised soberly. And it was as though all the ease was draining out of life. Everything was changing as she watched, but she could not tell whether this was because of actual material circumstances, or whether it was because she had grown up without realising it and now seemed to see everything five times as clearly—it was as though she had acquired several pairs of eyes instead of having to make do with one. Obviously a wide vision was a better thing to have than a narrow one. For all that, Jo did not by any means like everything she could now see.

7

Mostly Anthea

Jo had decided to beard Uncle Robert one afternoon when school was over. The summer term was well begun, so Oliver was away; she was sure he would have come with her if he had been about. It was his last term. In the autumn he would join Rose at the Technical College. It had been intended that he should remain another year at school and everyone confidently expected him to get a university place with ease. He had planned, in the interval, to do a spell of Voluntary Service Overseas. But he himself had worked out the new arrangement and pushed it through against considerable opposition. Oliver was well aware, as they all were, that his father might soon be out of a job. Continuing school fees would be a strain on the family resources, nor could the years at the university, grant or no grant, be easy for them. He would go to Barhampton daily, as Rose did, and live cheaply at home until he was qualified.

Jo asked Lydia to go with her to see Uncle Robert.

'He likes you, Lydia. You're much more his idea of what a girl should be than I am.'

'He likes Emily. Take her.'

'She's going swimming with Roland and the young twins, and they've promised to take Penny. Please come.'

'I'll come tomorrow.'

'But I've got my strength up today. You'd come if it was horses.'

'But it isn't horses. It's horses taking me home,' Lydia excused herself. 'I had a wonderful idea and Daddy's going to see if we can do it. I want to clean up the old stables and take one or two horses at livery—we've got masses of grazing. Then when I leave school I want to get a few hacks and give riding lessons. It was all planned that we'd discuss it together after school today.'

'Oh all right,' Jo said grudgingly. She was rather impressed to find Lydia being so practical about the future. But what a renegade the girl was! 'Horses! It's always horses with you. They're so old-fashioned.'

'They're so beautiful,' Lydia corrected her, smiling.

So Jo set out in search of Uncle Robert on her own.

When she was a hundred yards or so short of the Robert Towers' gate, she saw Anthea ahead of her, walking very slowly. The baby was due soon. Jo called out, and Anthea turned. She looked pale and tired, as though she had been surprised in her private grief and loneliness. She had told them hardly anything about her husband, only that he intended to be a teacher, while his parents wanted him to take over the family business; how his early marriage had added to their annoyance and disappointment, and in the midst of quarrels and wretchedness he had been drafted to fight in Vietnam . . . Now, in Anthea's face as she turned to Jo, there was somehow a reflection, a picture of the lost man.

The moment she saw Jo, Anthea tidied Paul away. 'This is my afternoon constitutional,' she said. 'Into the town, down the hill, along the river, up the hill. I get a cup of tea from Aunt Helen or Tamsin—then I totter home again the short way. All down hill. That part's nice.'

'It seems a long way,' said Jo. 'I mean—you know—just now.'

'Oh don't worry. There's always the telephone and the ambulance,' Anthea said, laughing.

They went into the house together. Meeting Anthea had removed Jo's sensation of approaching a formidable interview.

However, she need not have concerned herself about that at all, for Uncle Robert and Aunt Helen were both out. Only Tamsin was at home, and Adwoa was with her.

'They've gone to London,' Tamsin said. 'It's their wedding anniversary. They're going to the opera. They won't be back till tomorrow.'

The feeling of anti-climax made Jo groan. She flopped down on the enormous cushiony sofa under the window in the sitting-room, and Anthea carefully selected something more upright.

'Adwoa and I have been designing an outfit for a motoring honeymoon,' Tamsin told them. 'Don't you think that's rather specialised and marvellous?'

'But nothing is finished,' Adwoa said quickly, 'so it is not to be shown.'

'Can't they see the coat? That's done.'

'No. Nothing. We must finish the whole outfit.'

'We're having a partnership contest at the Art School,' Tamsin explained. 'It's much more difficult than designing on your own. Later on we've got to work as a team, four of us.'

'Goodness,' Jo said, 'the things you get up to. Give me a nice chassis to work on any day of the week.'

'Goodness,' mocked Adwoa, 'the things you get up to!'

They laughed together. Adwoa was wearing a dress she had designed and made for herself, and it had none of the extravagance of Tamsin's creations. It was a rich clear cherry that made her skin look smooth and blooming. Like Kojo, she had lovely hands, Jo noticed—a smaller, finer copy of his. But Kojo was twice as serious in manner. There was nothing flippant about Adwoa but she was easy and sure of her welcome. It was as though, for her, all the complications of the situation had been ironed out long ago.

'Telephone,' Jo said, hearing it ringing somewhere in another room.

'Let it ring,' said Tamsin.

Jo could never ignore a ringing bell and she did not want to do so now, even at second-hand.

'Perhaps it's your mother. Perhaps the car's broken down.'

'Of course it hasn't. It never does.'

'There's bound to be a first time.'

'Answer it yourself, then, if you're so bursting with curiosity,' Tamsin said.

'What shall I say if it's someone for Uncle Robert?'

'What can you say? You know perfectly well he isn't here.'

The bell had been ringing and ringing. Jo jumped up and ran out of the sitting-room, then remembered that the instrument was plugged in, in a grand fashion, wherever it was needed. So where was it now? She ran from room to room, feeling extremely foolish, but still finding time as she went to be awed by the conventional richness of the place. She found the telephone at last in the study on the right of the hall. She snatched up the receiver, thankful to be in time. To her astonishment Emily was at the other end.

'Jo—is it you? Anthea's there, isn't she?'

'Yes. What's the matter? Where are you? I thought you were swimming.'

'I'm at the Millers' now. There's nobody here but Roland and me and Penny. Uncle Brian's not back from work and Margaret's out with Rachel.'

'Well—go on. What is it?'

'Something's happened. You must tell Anthea.'

'What? *What?* You sound in an awful stew . . .'

'I am.'

'Go on, then—quick—tell me!'

'It's *Paul*, Jo. There's a cable. He's safe.'

'Safe . . . ?' Jo heard herself repeating what seemed an utterly meaningless word. 'Alive? *Alive?* Is that what it says?'

'Alive and well. It says *Safe and well* . . . They telephoned the cable and I took it down. It's *true*, Jo—not just me . . . You must tell Anthea.'

Jo panicked. 'I don't know how to . . . I can't . . .'

'Call her, then. Call her quickly. It's mad for us to know and not her.'

'Hang on . . .'

Jo put down the receiver. Her hands were sticky with excitement and fear. She was thinking, to her own surprise, of the baby—of how Anthea must not be shocked. But how could she fail to be? That the shock was a blessedly happy one had little to do with the case . . . Jo was shaking with nerves as she ran back into the sitting-room.

'It's for you, Anthea.'

'What's for me?' They had been talking, she and Tamsin and Adwoa, and had forgotten that Jo had run off to answer the telephone's ringing.

'Emily's on the telephone. Wants to speak to you.'

'She hasn't drowned Penny, has she?' Anthea said lazily, giving her deep laugh. Then, as she rose, she looked at Jo. Whatever she saw turned her pale. 'What's happened?' she cried, suddenly sharp. 'I *knew* they shouldn't have gone off swimming by themselves!'

'Nothing's happened to any of them,' Jo said, steadying. 'Nothing awful has happened at all, Anthea. It's something quite different—tremendous . . . Come and talk to Emily. She'll tell you.'

'Where is it? The telephone . . . ?'

'The study. On the right of the hall,' Tamsin said. She looked at Jo as Anthea went out of the room. 'What's happened?'

'Paul!' Jo said. 'Paul's happened! He's all right—he's alive . . .'

Adwoa moved past Jo instantly. She crossed the hall swiftly and lightly and reached the study just as Anthea dropped the telephone receiver and went to the ground as though she had been pole-axed, her head thudding on the splendidly polished boards where the fine thick carpet ended. The receiver hung dangling at the end of its flex, cracking and spitting for a second, then blanking into silence.

Jo and Tamsin took their orders from Adwoa. They put a cushion under Anthea's head and fetched an eiderdown to wrap round her. Adwoa patted her face briskly and pinched at her chin, then wrung out a cloth in cold water and laid it across her forehead. Anthea stirred and opened her eyes and lay there looking at the three of them in blank bewilderment. Adwoa was the stranger, but hers was the face in which Anthea read competence and authority, and it was to Adwoa she spoke.

'True?' she said. 'Is it true?'

'Yes,' said Adwoa. 'He is alive and well and will come home to you. Everything will be good now. Close your eyes and relax for a moment. Think about him quite slowly.'

'Never stopped,' murmured Anthea. But she closed her eyes as Adwoa had told her to, and for a second or two she was quite still, and they were all of them absolutely silent. Nothing stirred in the house, nothing sounded but a ticking clock. Outside, in a world that seemed so distant it had almost ceased to exist, a dog barked and barked, and cars passed the mouth of the drive, heard momentarily, then lost behind the high shrubbery that surrounded the house and garden. Then Anthea opened her eyes, and they were wide and dark, still looking to Adwoa for help. 'I'm afraid we've frightened the baby,' she said.

'Oh then, we'll ring up the hospital, shall we?' Adwoa said easily. 'Tamsin will do it. And let the doctor know, too. Can you think of his number?'

'I know it,' Tamsin said. 'This phone's broken now—I'll use the upstairs one. I hope that's all right.'

She ran off, and Jo would have been glad to follow her, but Adwoa needed help in getting Anthea to her feet. She was very shaky, and began to cry and laugh—not quite hysterically, but with the helplessness that might be expected of someone whose whole life has changed its course in a matter of seconds; and is still changing. Adwoa thought she should lie down, not on that billowy sofa but somewhere sensible. Jo remembered the little room off the kitchen where she had slept one Christmas Eve when the house was full for the family party, and all the young ones had been put to bed at Uncle Robert's. It was a plain room with a hard little bed, left over from the old days when servants were still to be had and the rich Robert Towers had not lacked them. As they helped Anthea on to the bed, which had nothing but a washed-out cotton cover on its thin mattress, Jo remembered hanging her Christmas stocking on the knob of the iron bedstead, and feeling it longingly in the dark night—the hard bits with edges, the soft bundles, the stuff of the stocking sliding and crunching on the paper wrappings, slithering over the orange in the toe . . .

Minutes passed and Tamsin had not reappeared. At last she came in looking extremely fussed.

'I haven't got through yet. The telephone's not working properly. I've tried the upstairs one, and I did get the exchange but I lost it again. The downstairs one's quite dead—I've tried it in other plugs, but it won't work.'

'Never mind,' said Adwoa, in that cool voice. 'Where's the nearest public call-box? Or the house next door? Why not try there?'

'The house next door's for sale. I'll run down to the corner of the square.' She dashed to the front door, then slid to a standstill and returned. 'Money.'

'Take my handbag,' said Adwoa.

Again Tamsin paused in the doorway. 'Is she all right?'

'Yes she is. Oh she *is*!' said Anthea, lying there with her eyes closed.

'Is the baby going to be born before the ambulance comes?'

'No, no,' said Adwoa. 'Not if you get along and call it soon. Go, Tamsin. Why have I worked to make myself a nurse if I cannot look after Anthea now?'

Tamsin went. Jo looked at Adwoa. Anthea was gripping her wrists and the pair of them were looking intently at one another, an immediate, necessary partnership from which Jo knew herself altogether excluded. She went and stood in the doorway, hearing them talking together. She tried to imagine what it must be like for Anthea, suddenly knowing that she was no longer alone, that the baby was not after all to grow up without a father. But it was too big, too personal. All she could think of was that the baby was still locked up in the dark and must somehow make its way into the world. She leant against the doorway, quaking to recall that this simplest and most ordinary of processes could none the less be disastrous. Then Adwoa's matter-of-fact voice woke her up and she felt instantly ashamed of her fears.

'Shall we have a cup of tea? Will you make it, Jo?'

While Jo was filling the kettle, Tamsin came back. She had got through to the hospital and the ambulance was on its way. It arrived before the kettle had boiled.

'I'll go with her,' Adwoa said. 'Will one of you fetch her things from home? Her bag's packed, she says. Please bring it to the hospital.'

'I'll bring it,' Jo said. She watched as Anthea was helped into the ambulance. The doors closed, the wheels spat sedately on the gravel drive, the ambulance moved off at once, slid through the gateway and vanished.

'Not even using the siren,' Jo complained.

'Shall we drink the tea?' Tamsin asked.

'Better collect her bag and get it to the hospital. She won't have even a comb or a nightie until we do.'

'Somehow I feel like a mother-in-law,' said Tamsin. She sat down on a kitchen chair and most unexpectedly began to cry. So Jo poured out the tea after all, speaking firmly but kindly to Tamsin, in a manner she thought might be a fair copy of Adwoa's.

'I hope Adwoa's around the next time anyone has a baby, that's all,' Jo said. 'Suppose you really hadn't brought her home—just as I told you not to. We'd have looked pretty silly, wouldn't we?'

'Perhaps I'll be a nurse after all,' Tamsin said, sniffing and blowing her nose. 'Will you?'

'No, of course I won't. Nor will you. Do pull yourself together, Tam,' said Jo, her spirits bounding up to normal now that Anthea was safely out of the way. 'Come on and collect that suitcase.'

'You,' said Tamsin, leaning back in her chair and yawning . . .

Jo took the short way to the Millers'—all down hill, as Anthea had said. When she got there the place was in a turmoil, for Margaret had returned with Rachel and had just read the cable. *Paul safe and well. With you earliest.* It was signed *Mom.*

'Now everything's going to be all right!' cried Emily, who had stayed behind to keep Penny company after Roland and the other two boys went home. 'Now Anthea will just *have* to be nice to them . . .'

'Oh I'd so much like Paul to get here before the baby!' Margaret said. 'With such a shock as this it might all happen so quickly. Oh I'd like him to be here in time!'

'Don't worry. He will be,' said Emily.

Jo glared at her. 'You said you'd grown out of that sort of thing.'

'Well, you just see if I'm right,' said Emily. She was standing by the window and had already seen the car at the gate. A long, lean young man with very short hair uncoiled himself from the driving seat.

'There you are,' said Emily, as the door bell rang. 'What did I say?'

'What was gorgeous,' Jo said afterwards to Lydia, 'was that the moment we all looked at him—the very second we saw his face—we knew that Anthea had been a clever chooser.'

He had stepped inside the house and stood on the mat, stooping to speak to Margaret, who was barely up to his shoulder.

'Excuse me, ma'am,' he said, 'but I think you have my wife.'

Margaret said, 'I'm her stepmother. I'm the only mother-in-law you're going to get. Oh Paul!' And she threw her arms round him and hugged him and wept. 'We've only just had the cable from your mother—not much more than an hour ago. Oh I can't believe it!'

'Oh,' he said. He patted Margaret kindly and gently, smiling over her head at Rachel, who was dancing about in her excitement. Then his glance swept over the rest of them. 'Anthea?' he asked.

Both Jo and Emily were bursting to tell him, but it seemed to be Margaret's job.

'Tell him! Tell him!' shrieked Rachel. 'I'm going to be an aunt!' she told Paul.

'Then you're Rachel, and you're the youngest. And that one's Penny, isn't it? Penny—you look a sensible sort of woman, so tell me where I can find your sister Anthea.'

Margaret broke in, then. 'The baby's on the way, Paul. When the news came—well, I suppose it couldn't wait any longer. Jo can tell you—this is Jo—she was there and helped get an ambulance and everything.'

'Thanks,' said Paul. He set Margaret aside and took Jo by the wrist. 'You come right along *now* and show me the way to the hospital. I'll see you later, mother-in-law.' And grinning at Margaret, and still hanging on to Jo, he strode out of the house.

'The bag!' Jo cried. 'Emily—give me Anthea's bag with her things in!'

Emily dashed down the path with the suitcase and thrust it into the car after them.

'Now,' said Paul, as he settled his long legs with some difficulty in the small hired car. 'She's all right, isn't she? Nothing alarming? Not an emergency?'

'Only you. I'd call you an emergency. Anthea just sort of swooned with joy. Adwoa coped.'

'Who's she?'

'A great friend of Tamsin's. A trained nurse. She comes from Ghana.' As she spoke Jo looked at him quickly and closely.

'And Tamsin . . . Don't tell me. She's the second daughter of Robert Tower, and he's the head of the family. Her sister's called Camilla and she's gotten herself a husband named Alan something. Correct? I've done a lot of homework on this subject.'

'Where've you been? What happened to you?'

'Mostly fever. Bit of a wound. Hid up in the jungle. I was lucky
—cared for by some wonderful people. As soon as may be I was
on my way back to base. Then Saigon. Cabled Anthea and got a
reply *Gone Away*. Cabled my folks and got a reply *Gone to England*.
Didn't take long to arrange leave. I hopped a plane—Red Cross—
and got here before I knew it . . . How's she been, Jo?'

'Terrific,' said Jo.

'What's that mean—in this context?'

'Brave, I suppose.'

'How far now?' he asked.

They were coming up to the hospital as he spoke. Jo led Paul
inside and the first person she saw was Adwoa, talking with one of
the senior nurses.

'I guessed you'd be coming with the bag. So I waited around.'

'This is Paul,' Jo said. 'Paul, this is our friend Adwoa.'

She was praying that the meeting would be all right, and she
thought probably the nurse standing with Adwoa was doing the
same. Paul held out his hand. 'Jo's been telling me. Thanks for
everything you did.' He looked at the nurse. 'I'd like to see her
please.'

'Go and sit down in the waiting-room,' said the nurse, making it
clear that this was her hospital, not theirs. 'I'll enquire.'

They sat down as she had commanded.

'Distract me,' suggested Paul. 'Tell me everything Anthea has
done and said since she came back to England.'

There was plenty of time. The nurse stayed away and stayed
away. Jo told all she could think of about Anthea; Adwoa described
in detail, several times, how Emily had telephoned the cable and
what had happened then. The trolley came round and they drank
cups of coffee that made Paul grimace. The trolley came round
again and he drank tea—and still grimaced. The nurse appeared
and they all leapt up—but she only paused to put her head round
the door and say that she was still finding out if he could see
Anthea.

'Honestly!' cried Jo. She was getting exceedingly hungry and wondered what on earth they must be thinking at home. She looked helplessly at Adwoa, but she was settling down again patiently.

'I guess this comes of being a father,' Paul said, seizing what hair he had and tugging it with both hands. 'Go on, Jo. Keep on talking.'

This time Jo told about Tower Motors, the take-over by C.M.H. and the general misery it had caused the family. She described every Tower and every Tower's appearance. She spoke of the veteran cars, the fears for their future, the trouble between Kojo and the other apprentices—leaving out Rose's part in the business. She lost count of how long they had been there—sometimes the clock seemed to have leapt on, sometimes it seemed to have stopped.

'And now,' said Paul, suddenly rising up to his great height, 'I propose to pull this building apart until I find what I'm looking for. *I've stood enough!*'

As he strode to the door, another strange nurse appeared.

'Sister,' said Adwoa.

'And I don't suppose you're the only one, Mr Darrell,' said the sister. 'You *are* Mr Darrell?'

'I am Mr Darrell—'

'Come this way, then, will you?'

'Is she all right? Is she all right?'

'Of course she's all right. Wouldn't you be? When she woke up this morning she was a widow—now she's got a husband and a daughter . . .'

'Have a heart,' Paul said. 'Let's go!' But he was grinning now and looked as if he would kiss the nurse rather than strangle her.

'Had to keep you waiting,' Sister said. 'You understand, don't you? She had a great shock. Wonderful—but a great shock. We had to take care. Now—come along and see her. But only five minutes.'

They were gone and Jo and Adwoa stood looking after them.

'Glorious,' said Adwoa. 'It's so glorious—all of it. So they have a daughter.'

Jo thought she sounded a bit disappointed over that part of the glorious business, and she bristled in the baby's defence.

'I'm glad it's a girl. Camilla has a boy.' She looked at Adwoa. 'I must say you look quite starry-eyed, even if it isn't a son. How many babies get born in this hospital every day?'

'Oh—I don't know. Lots, I daresay.'

'Then why are we making such a fuss about this one?' Jo demanded. 'It's bound to be hideous.'

Adwoa looked at Jo and laughed. Rather slyly, Jo thought.

Patricia Margaret became Meg almost before the first creases had smoothed out of her red and worried face. The excitement over Paul's miraculous return fizzed through the family. Literally fizzed, for Uncle Robert and Aunt Helen gave a party the moment Anthea was well enough to attend, and much champagne was drunk and spilt. The cares of the Towers were forgotten for a few hours in the general rejoicing. Camilla and Alan came, bringing James, no longer *the* family baby. Even Uncle Saville, Jo's Uncle Saville, was invited, which showed how big-hearted Uncle Robert was feeling, for he looked upon Saville as a loafer and a waster. Aunt Silly Milly was there, out for the day, with Miss Surplice, both wearing black hats and black stockings in mourning for Aunt Harriet, and Adwoa and Kojo came, too. It was a day to remember—a big day. Hugh and Robin rushed from Cambridge, Oliver cycled the twelve miles from his school, Sukey arrived in a small and dashing motor-car driven by a young and dashing man. 'Oh—only Miranda's brother,' she said carelessly, naming a fellow pupil and dismissing her escort with a flippant wave of the hand.

'Pick you up at six!' he shouted as he moved off.

Sukey waved the other hand and went into the house, flicking a large-eyed glance at Tamsin as they passed on the steps.

It was a Sunday in late May and the summer had really begun. The garden shone in its well-kept glory—the shrubs at their best, a blaze of crimson, purple, orange, yellow, sugar-pink. The scent of the azaleas was sharp as citron, yet heavy as cloves, drifting in great waves as the sun warmed it, as the light breeze puffed it about the garden and through the house. They were all—the less fortunate, if that was the word—inclined to laugh at the Robert Towers, with their conventional comfort, their rich display. But their parties were generous and easy to enjoy. That day was the day to watch Paul loitering about among them, eyeing them, learning them, looking for Anthea a little desperately at times, needing an interpreter when the family language became over-obscure.

'Does he like us?' Lydia asked Jo, as they leant side by side on the pretty little iron balustrade outside the drawing-room windows. Below them on the lawn the party moved gaily in the sunshine. Lunch was over and there was coffee being served from a table under the cherry trees.

'Why shouldn't he like us?'

'He might not. Some don't.'

'But some must, Lydia. Why not Paul? Don't be so humble.'

'I'm not. I quite wish his rich snobby relations were here.'

'Do you? I don't. Why?'

Lydia laughed. 'Just to show them Anthea's got some, too, I suppose!'

'Okay—you're not humble after all. Now I'd never say a thing like that. I'd even try not to think it.'

They both exploded into convulsive laughter. The tears stood in Lydia's eyes and Jo's face turned bright pink. Once they had started they could not stop—they were back in their youngest days when they had watched Clive and the Miller twins smoking secretly down by the river, keeping themselves hidden and nearly bursting with laughter at the ludicrous sight.

'What's so funny?' asked Paul, coming up behind them and grinning sympathetically at their convulsions.

'Everything!' Lydia managed. 'But mostly *us*.'

'You're all right.'

'That's what we were wondering,' Jo told him. 'Lydia said, "Does he like us?" That's you. Do you?'

He answered her in a replica of Anthea's drawl—'I think you're *fabulous*.'

'Oh,' said Jo.

She sounded so disappointed that he was the one who laughed then. He put an arm round the waist of each girl and hugged them. 'I mean it! I mean it! You gorgeous girls—you're my in-laws and I can kiss you all as much as I like in a good in-lawly way. Jo and Lydia—Tamsin and Sukey, Rose, Emily, Penny, Rachel. None shall say me Nay!'

Anthea called him from somewhere across the lawn.

'He dropped us and ran,' said Lydia. 'Anthea's jolly lucky.'

'Now,' said Jo. 'She's lucky now.'

They stayed together a little longer, looking out over the garden, picking out the members of the family and remarking on their clothes. Aunt Lucy was wearing a hideous dress that would make Oliver cringe, for he liked his mother to look elegant; and so she did about once in a dozen occasions. Uncle Peter Cardew wore an embroidered waistcoat, Auntie Jay was in heavy white silk, entirely plain—more rich relations for Paul, though certainly not 'rich snobby' as Lydia had called the Robert Towers. Among the considerable throng, Kojo walked with Adwoa.

'Don't you think it must seem rather imperialistic to those two, Lydia? A garden party at the residency—or whatever it was called.'

Emily had come along the verandah towards them.

'Ask her. She'll know,' said Lydia.

But Jo did not want to repeat what she had said. She looked down again on the crowded lawns. A score of strange unnameable fears flooded her mind. The picture she had imagined for Kojo increased and re-shaped itself. Not only a garden party at the residency, she thought, but the eve of Waterloo, the sinking of the *Titanic*, the massacre of St Bartholomew. This was the scene, of crowding revelry, that played itself out right through history on the eve of disasters and farewells.

Unauthorised Persons

The next time Jo attempted to see Uncle Robert, Emily went, too. Emily now had a bicycle, so they cycled round by the river and along the tow path, then pushed up the steep hill to the house.

'I don't suppose it'll be as exciting as it was last time,' Emily said, remembering how once before they had been to see Uncle Robert in his grand office, to ask if the old cars might be used in the festival at Milsom Magnificorum.

'It'll be terrifying,' Jo said soberly. 'I never stop being frightened of Uncle Robert.'

'Perhaps he'll be easier to talk to now he's retired. Lots of time to himself and no worries,' Emily said.

'I wish I had no worries. I'm more worried than I've ever been in my life.' Jo gave a great sigh and seemed to look back over the long weary years of her existence like some old crone at a tumble-down cottage door. 'All right—laugh. This is a horrible term for me. I'm no good at exams at any time—but this time is hopeless. I dreadfully want to do well—I ought to be mugging away at maths at this very moment. Lydia's bound to get through everything, she always does. The awful thing is she's really only interested in certificates about riding and stable management. What a waste!'

Emily looked at Jo as they puffed up the steep hill together, and thought how she had changed lately. Her manner had always been positive, to say the very least, but it was losing its noisy assertiveness and becoming much more reasoned. Nothing was likely to diminish Jo's passionate enthusiasm for the things she cared about, but it was as though these things were toughening and thickening inside her and giving her confidence in her own opinions—so that she no longer needed to shout them to the world. Emily was not precisely aware of the processes at work, but she appreciated the result. Within this last year of her growing, Jo had become twice as kind. She had allowed herself to accept Emily, then to enjoy her; and she worked hard to make Kojo one of them, though only partially successfully. In any conflict between her and Emily, Jo would win her point far more subtly than she could have done even three or four months ago. Where she had banged and bellowed, she now dug in her toes and stood her ground. Later, no doubt, she would discover how to do this and still smile disarmingly in the face of an opponent. It was a little as though her clash with the boys at the works—which Emily had heard about from Roland, who had had it from an appreciative Gilbert—had been the last wild fling of the child in Jo. Even as little later as this, she would have handled the business differently.

As for the outward signs of change in Jo, even young Penny might have noticed those. She was growing fussy about her hair, impatient with her clothes, and when she used a bit of make-up she took time enough to use it well. Her Uncle Saville, who had annoyed her by calling her 'a good-looker' in a somewhat dated way, had in fact been perfectly right.

'One of my worries is you,' Jo told Emily.

'I suppose you mean Aunt Sam? Well, I can't help going to stay with her, I expect. I don't want to. If I've got to go away I'd much rather go to Ghana and stay with the Amponsahs. I want to see *that* baby, too. Anyway, it's only for the summer holidays, Jo.'

Summer arrangements throughout the family had been greatly upset by the situation over Tower Motors. During the period of take-over it was essential that those concerned should be at hand. Uncle Robert's quick and discreet retirement had brought in a new chairman and managing director and by the autumn the new regime would be in control—there were already many changes. Because of all this, the Cardews were not going to France, the Millers had cancelled a fortnight in Cornwall. The Evenses and the David Towers had been going to Scotland together, which would have pleased Jo, but that was off, too. The Holt parents hardly ever went away because it was so difficult to leave the farm—Clive intended camping in the Lake District, and would probably take Roland along, but Lydia was happy to stay at home because of her own plans and the work entailed.

'What am I supposed to say to Uncle Robert?' Emily asked, as she and Jo turned in at the gate.

'I'm sure you'll know when the time comes. Until then, just look hideously girlish.'

'Shall I undo my hair?' It was tied in a pony tail and she did look rather skinned, so Jo thought this might be a good idea. Emily had a comb in her saddle bag and they slid into hiding and attended to the matter. They emerged in a rather giggling condition and tried to sober up as they finished the last lap up the tidy gravel drive to the impressive porticoed door.

Uncle Robert was in the garden, surprisingly in filthy old trousers and a sports shirt with a tear under one arm, halfway up a ladder set against the back of the house, giving the wisteria its summer pruning.

'Robert, you have callers,' said Aunt Helen, who had ushered the two girls outside. 'Jo and Emily, dear. They'd like a word with you.'

He looked down at them without any great enthusiasm. 'I suppose you think as I'm a retired old man I've no work to do. Well—as you can see—you are quite wrong.'

'We'll come back another time,' said Jo, glad of a chance to retreat.

'No, no—of course you won't. I shall be just as busy then.' He came slowly down the ladder and stood pulling off his gloves. He changed his glasses and then seemed to see the girls more clearly. He asked what he could do for them.

'Something I wanted to ask you about the old cars, Uncle Robert.'

'Oh good gracious, Josephine—you're forever bullying me about the old cars. What is it this time?'

'Whose are they?'

Jo had intended a more diplomatic approach, but Robert Tower's manner told her it would make little difference how she came to the point, so she came to it directly.

'Whose are they?' he repeated.

'Who do they belong to? I mean—now.'

'One of the boys was asking me that the other day. I believe it was your young brother Roland.'

'What did you tell him?' Obviously nothing, both Jo and Emily realised, or Roland would have been bursting with his privately gained information.

'Look, Jo, I know you feel some fondness for the collection—'

'Fondness, Uncle Robert? We work on them nearly every week. There isn't a piece of them, engine or body work, that isn't clean and shining and in perfect order. You could start up any one of them and drive it right away. You can't have seen them lately, or you'd know.'

'I didn't say anything about their condition, or how it comes about, my dear. I am very well aware that you young people have put in many hours of excellent work.' He was sounding more human now. He sat down on a nearby stone bench and put his hands on his knees. 'However, it must be obvious to you that since they are housed on Tower Motors ground, and are part of the whole concern, they now belong to County Mechanical Holdings.'

For a second Jo was silent. This confirmation of all their worst fears was a most appalling blow. She was not even prepared at first to accept or believe it.

'My grandfather collected them,' she said at last.

'Yes, indeed, poor old George, they were his joy—his treasure. But when he died they were not specially provided for. He did not even mention them in his will—which was a remarkable document, anyway. He put back into the firm everything he considered he had taken out. If he hadn't done that, your father would be a very wealthy man.'

Jo began again, from a slightly different angle. 'Don't you remember how we all wanted to have a Tower Transport Museum, Uncle Robert? We told you all about it that time we asked for the cars—to drive in the festival at Milsom Magnificorum. You remember, don't you?'

'I remember very well. They looked excellent. And were well driven. Everyone was most impressed. It was a good idea of yours. And splendidly contrived, I have to admit, by your Uncle Saville.'

'Well, then,' said Jo, as though she had proved something.

For the first time, he looked at her directly. For the first time, too, she saw what this business had done to him. Somehow whenever they said to one another 'We're all in it together', they had rather inclined to leave out Uncle Robert. He seemed so safe, so comfortable, so aloof. Now in his slightly flinching gaze, in the old man's grey eyes that had replaced those of a keen executive, she saw how deeply all this had struck at him. It was a polite fiction to say that he had retired—his life's work had been snatched from him.

'My dear,' he said, 'try to understand that when a firm is taken-over, bought-up, whatever you like to call it, all its assets are included. What good would it have been to say: But we'll keep the shed with the veteran cars, because that's a private matter. It's on your ground, because you've paid for it, but it's ours, just the same . . . You can't do that sort of thing.'

'But if the cars are yours,' Emily suggested, speaking for the first time, 'just the cars, I mean—you can take them away and put them somewhere else.'

'Of course!' Jo cried, delighted with Emily. 'Somewhere in the town. There's the old chapel in Cross Street. It's been up for sale for years so it's sure to be going cheap. Why couldn't we use that?'

'You must try to understand, both of you,' he said, sounding sterner and far less agreeable, hating them, perhaps, for forcing him to put all this into words, 'that the whole of Tower Motors, lock, stock and barrel, has passed out of my hands and out of the hands of every single one of us. Those of us who remain are employees, subject to the whim of the employer. Accept it, as I have had to do . . . Now you must go, because I want to finish this pruning job.'

The following weekend Oliver was home from school. Examinations were due to start almost immediately and this clear weekend was intended to refresh what he called his weary spirit and over-burdened mind. It was he who suggested that Paul Darrell should be taken to see the old cars for he was not likely to be in Milsom Parva much longer; he had already made one trip home. Oliver had arranged this with Paul before he telephoned Jo. After a second's hesitation, Jo said nothing about the visit to Uncle Robert. The take-over was not yet complete, so she could see no reason for keeping off long familiar ground. Gilbert had certainly made no objection to their usual Saturday morning activities, and he was still in authority in his own department whatever might have happened to his late bosses. Anyway, Jo felt that C.M.H. had better get accustomed to the young Towers, who could not be without their uses, and who were surely still entitled to some consideration. As she thought this, she knew already she was backing a horse with at least one broken leg, but she was not prepared to admit the fact. *Accept it as I have had to,* Uncle Robert had said. She was nowhere near being able to do so.

Paul fetched Jo from home and they went to the Evenses' house in The Crescent to collect Oliver. Emily and Roland had set off together half an hour before. It was Kojo's morning off from work, but Jo felt he should be with them—however, Emily had assured her that he had something else to do, though she didn't say what.

'You've got a nice little town here,' Paul was saying, as they moved slowly through the High Street shoppers on their way to The Crescent. 'Anthea tells me it's not the place it was. But I like it.'

'Stay, then,' she urged.

'I've got work to do. And there's my family. I want to show them Anthea and the baby and see we all get friendly again. But we'll be back, Jo. What do you think? Anyway—don't you want to come visiting in the States?'

'Oh I'd love to come—oh I would!' Jo cried. 'Relations in America! I've only just thought—how *useful*—how *wonderful!*'

They had paused at a pedestrian crossing, and Paul looked sideways at her and laughed at her eagerness. Then as they moved off, he said, 'There's the little nurse, look. I'll be grateful to that girl till my dying day.'

Adwoa had just crossed ahead of them. She was swinging along laughing at the young man beside her. The young man was Kojo, and he was laughing, too—a Kojo gay and easy as they had hardly ever seen him. Jo was already winding down the window to call out to the pair when she noticed that they were walking along hand in hand.

'Look at that, Paul!'

'Look at what?'

'Holding hands. Adwoa and Kojo.'

'What's so odd? They're two of a kind and easy together. She's a nice girl. And he's not a bad guy, either. We've had them both in for a meal several evenings.'

'I thought he'd been to night classes.'

Paul grinned. 'Well, in a way, I guess that's what we offered. He's loosened up a lot since I first met him.'

All Jo could think of in the way of an objection was, 'He's younger than she is.' Just as she had said of Kojo and Rose.

'That's true. But she's only a kid. I know she's done three years' nursing, but that includes pupil-nursing. Kojo's years old for his age, wouldn't you say? My guess is they like being together quite a lot.'

'Does—' Jo had been going to say, *Does Rose know?* but she changed it. 'Does Emily know?' If so, she had been most abominably secretive. And so she might have been, for she was on the defensive over Kojo. He had somehow not quite become absorbed into their community as they had all been so determined that he should. Too determined? Too self-consciously determined, perhaps.

When they reached the Evenses' house, there was Oliver with his head under the bonnet of the family car.

Jo called out, 'What's wrong?'

'Absolutely nowt,' he called back, deeply disappointed. He flung down the bonnet in disgust and stalked towards them, shaking his head and pushing at his spectacles. Next to Paul, he looked rather long-haired. 'Things are coming to a pretty pass,' he complained, 'when your own father's car is in perfect condition.'

'Too bad,' said Paul.

'It is. I rely on him to mess up the engine the moment I'm out of the way. Then I can have the pleasure of putting it right. So it is too bad. Specially as we're not going to have any others to work on, by all accounts.'

Jo's cold voice sounded from a great distance in her own ears. 'Whose accounts?'

'Be your age, Jo. We've lost Tower Motors. Who's going to let us in to mess about the way we always have done?'

'Gilbert will. Gilbert's still general foreman.'

'It's not our place any more. We've discussed all this, Jo.'

'We haven't discussed never going to work there on Saturdays.'

'Because it's obvious. Nothing to discuss.'

'Where now?' asked Paul, cutting in.

Jo said, 'Left, then right, then second left,' and sank into silence again. This short and familiar journey was becoming altogether too disturbing.

When they came to the works entrance they found Rose, Emily and Roland talking to the man at the gate. Old Walter

Greenway had been on the gate for years, but this was a much younger man, with a shock of dark hair and a rather red face.

'George Daley—isn't it?' Oliver said.

'Yes, it is. Where's Walter, then?'

Roland broke away from the group at the gate and came up to the car as Jo and Oliver got out. 'He won't let us in, Jo.'

Jo did not answer him. She walked up to the gate without waiting for Oliver, who was telling Paul where to park. Rose was standing with her hands in her pockets, leaning against the closed gates. She was pale and her eyes had the glitter that went with a rising passion of rage. Emily looked relieved when Jo approached. She opened her mouth to speak, then closed it again because Jo passed by without a word. When she reached the gates she said cheerfully—'Oh, there you are, Rose. You've just beaten me to it. I'm sorry I'm late.' Then she looked at the man on duty and said, 'Hullo, George. How's Mavis?'

'She's fine, thanks,' replied George. He smiled at Jo, but he looked unhappy. 'We're all in trouble here,' he said.

'Darling George won't let us in,' said Rose, in a voice like the tinkle of ice.

George got redder than ever and began to look downright miserable. 'They put me on this job,' he said, 'and they told me what to do.'

'Where's Walter?'

'Gone. Redundant. Well—a bit old, they said.'

'There's a new notice, Jo,' Emily put in.

Sure enough, there it was, painted black on white, neat, clean and uncompromising. *No Entry for Unauthorised Persons.*

Jo was aware of two things—her own need to keep calm, and the fact that Oliver had moved in behind her and might speak before she did. This was not what she wanted.

She laughed—and it sounded quite easy and natural, not at all as if she was having difficulty with her breathing because her heart was pounding like a steam hammer.

'Oh—that,' she said.

She felt rather than heard Oliver choke back whatever he had been going to say. She saw the quick close attention of the others focused on her, waiting for her to deal with this because they saw she had a way of which they knew nothing at all.

'We're only going through to the old cars, George,' she said. 'This is Mr Darrell with us. He's American—well, I'm sure you know all about him—and he's particularly interested in old things.'

'Oh,' said George. He looked at Paul with interest, even excitement, for the tale of the soldier's return to his young wife at the very moment that his daughter was being born had not unnaturally been told a hundred times about the town. 'Look—I'll have to check it. I'm sorry about this. Give me a second and I'll ring through and ask.'

'That's all right,' said Jo, still smiling. 'I've already got the key.' And she pulled it out of her pocket and wagged it cheerfully.

The others were still and watchful, but George was greatly relieved.

'Oh well, then, that's that, isn't it? Come on through.'

He opened the gates, and in they went, Paul last and wearing a slightly bewildered expression.

'Poor old Walter,' Jo stopped to say, enjoying herself too much not to push her luck a bit.

'You've said it,' George agreed. 'What a change, eh?'

'*Change and decay in all around I see,*' said Jo, in a brisk and disapproving voice.

'That's right,' agreed George, more fervently than the first time . . .

Jo let them all into the shed, then closed the door.

'Hats off,' said Rose, calm again. 'Where did you get the key?'

'I hung on to it, weeks ago. I just somehow felt we might need it.' She sat down on the nearest running-board and put her head in her hands. 'How does it feel to the rest of you—being an unauthorised person?'

'Stinking,' said Rose.

'What are we going to do now?' demanded Roland.

'There isn't much we can do, is there?' Oliver answered him. All these years we've had what we wanted and now we've got to do without. It's just too simple.'

'Well, all right—I can see they might turn us out of the repair shop and that sort of thing,' said Rose. 'What makes me spit is the idea of keeping us out of here. These are our cars. We've looked after them for years now. They're ours.'

'Uncle Robert let them go with everything else,' Jo cried. 'I think he must have been mad. How could he? And what have they got to do with County Mechanical Holdings, really? What use are they—except to us?'

Paul had been listening all this time without comment. 'Of course they're of use,' he said now. 'Valuable—beautiful—rare.' He began walking around the nearest model, an old high Buick with enormous wheels. 'If you want them, why shouldn't others? Dear knows what they'd fetch in the open market.'

'Fetch? Are you suggesting they might be sold?' That was Rose, still using her glacial voice, so that Paul grimaced and put up a hand as if to ward off a blow. She laughed briefly at that. 'Well, seriously, Paul—'

'I am serious. You know as well as I do there's an international market for this sort of thing. I can think of half a dozen rich guys who'd fly the Atlantic to be at the sale. I don't know anything about the new regime here. But they're not members of the family, that's certain, and it's not all that likely that they're soft-centred sentimentalists. They'll have a different way of looking at things.' He shook his head and ran a hand over the bright bonnet of the Buick. 'I'd have expected the old man to hang on to this much, I must say.'

'I asked my father about it,' Oliver told him. 'Dad says he thinks Uncle Robert meant to keep the collection in the first place, but the way the deal went and the way the contract was drawn up put him off. He just threw in his hand and got out.'

'Now there can never be a Tower Transport Museum,' Jo

mourned. 'It was going to be absolutely smashing, Paul. I've got all these and more in miniature—I've got exactly four hundred and ninety-nine tiny cars and I always imagined them in a lovely glass case in the entrance hall.'

'It's a real sell-out, Jo.'

'If only I was twenty-one,' Emily said, 'I might be rich enough to buy them. Suppose they're still here . . . Oh it's not for ages. What a hope.'

Jo and Oliver flicked a rather shamefaced glance at one another, knowing very well that they had already decided between them how Emily should employ her fortune when the time came. Anyway, this quick and generous expression of her complete involvement was heartening. They all revived a little, warmed by what she had said.

They had brought Paul to see the cars, and whatever the circumstances now appeared to be there was no reason in the world why they should deny themselves the pleasure of showing him round. So they took him from car to car, opening this and pointing out that, urging him into the driving seat of the Hispano Suiza of 1911—he knew about the famous T-head engine, which sent him up even higher in their regard. They encouraged him to inspect the underneath of the 60-year-old Lanchester—in fact Rose squirmed underneath with him to point out the peculiarities of the steering. They lay side by side looking, Oliver said, like a grasshopper and an ant, earnestly discussing splendid technicalities. They showed him the three-cylinder Lea-Francis, the glorious Lagonda, younger by years, but still a proud possession. Then they came to the special built by old George Tower two years before he died. Its built-in luxuries remained absolutely pristine, for he had been ashamed of the pretentious cocktail cabinet and the little dressing-cupboard with gold-topped bottles that he had designed for his wife. These things had never been used. Except that the scent bottle in the dressing-cupboard was full, everything else was as clean as on the day it had been fitted. Jo opened the scent bottle—'It belonged to my grandmother, after all'—and dabbed some on Rose and Emily and herself. Shut up for all those years, it seemed at first to smell of nothing at all. Then gradually it warmed on their skin and a faint odour of flowers, perhaps wall-flowers, wafted about the shed that was more accustomed to the utilitarian smells of petrol and oil, leather and polish. Emily closed her eyes and sniffed.

'Do you remember her, Jo?'

'I'm pretending I remember she smelt of wallflowers,' Jo said honestly. Then she looked at Emily and said quickly, 'Don't start anything, for goodness' sake. We've got enough to cope with. We don't want ghosts as well.'

'All right,' said Emily, opening her eyes.

'Emily used to be a seer,' Jo told Paul, emphasising *used*. 'Now she only pretends. Don't you, Emily?'

'Hm, hm,' said Emily, pursing up her mouth, 'I can tell you she went driving in a sable stole.'

'There's nothing smart in that. Aunt Ruth's still got it—Lydia told you.'

'Perhaps she did,' said Emily, 'and perhaps she didn't.'

'He must have been a grand old boy, Jo,' Paul said, sitting at the wheel and looking with admiration over the big car's interior. 'And what he didn't know about a motor car!'

'He spoke good Dorset till the day he died,' Jo told Paul, 'and the others used to get mad with him. I suppose it was a bit of an affectation, really. But it meant he got on frightfully well with all the men in the works. Daddy always says the brothers were jealous of him. They'd worked so hard to turn themselves into gentlemen—but he was really the successful one.'

They were standing in a group round Paul now, and each of them had something to say to him.

'Isn't it maddening for me,' Rose said, 'I'm so terribly on the distaff side. I haven't been Tower for two generations.'

'What about you, Oliver?' Paul said. 'You're on the distaff side, too. Don't tell me, please. Your mother and Emily's father were brother and sister. How's that?'

'You are worthy,' said Roland. He meant exactly that, but it sounded terrible in every way, and he went scarlet and got inside one of the cars in his embarrassment.

'And my mother,' said Emily, who had never before mentioned her, never used the word *mother* at all since she got to Milsom Parva, 'was American. So you and I are almost relations—aren't we, Paul?'

'Indeed, we almost are. And a very fine thing, too, ma'am, if I may make so bold.'

Of course Roland was absolutely right—he *was* worthy. Camilla's Alan was good enough, but he had been known to patronise the least bit—though Camilla said that was just his Highland pride. If only Paul and Anthea could settle down in Milsom Parva, what a fine addition to family affairs that might mean . . . But there Jo paused. She could not go on to say, *And he should have a job with Tower Motors*. And this check to her imagining led to another. For she suddenly thought of such a job as Paul might fill, but which now would fall to some other applicant, perhaps a local man whose need was real and urgent. Towers for Tower Motors . . . Had they almost eaten up the locality in the days of their greatest prosperity? Had it ever been said—Not a chance to get in, except on the shop floor . . . Towers take the best . . . ? What they wanted to take now, she saw with alarming clarity, was the shop floor, too. They were being prevented from this. No—not prevented, that was not the right word. It was simply that they would now be obliged to approach what they wanted along conventional, competitive lines. The tower that was the family, the tower that Jo since childhood had seen as a build-up like that of acrobats in a circus standing on one another's shoulders, began as she considered it to sway and shift. The balance was upset. Individuals moved to the ground, not exactly falling, but relinquishing their reliance one on the other. As they levelled out, she saw with relief that they still hung on to one another by the hand, strung into a long chain that must not, that would not break . . .

The twelve o'clock noises over Milsom Parva roused Jo, roused all of them. It was time to leave.

'Let's wait for Kojo,' Rose said, as they walked across the yard to the gates. 'I can give him a lift home.'

'He's not working this Saturday,' Emily said, clearly and concisely.

Rose looked slightly annoyed, as though she had been caught out in tiresome ignorance. 'I quite forgot he had the morning off.'

'Alternate Saturdays. He and Adwoa have gone shopping.'

Jo was ahead, but she heard Emily clearly, and as clearly Rose's quick reply—'Kojo and *who?*'

'Adwoa. They were going to buy a picnic and catch the bus to the sea.'

'Well, let's hope it keeps fine for them,' said Rose, sharply and vulgarly.

By now they had reached the gates, through which the Saturday staff, a lot less than half the usual force, was pushing for home. George looked out at the young Towers and called—'Okay?'

'Yes, thanks,' Jo called back, nodding and smiling in the friendliest possible fashion. 'Mr Darrell was very interested.'

'Sure,' agreed Paul. 'A very fine collection. Thanks for letting me in.'

'That's all right,' said George. He shouted after Jo, who was now outside the gates, 'What about the key?'

'I'll look after that,' she said cheerfully—and truthfully. She waved it over her head, then as she passed out of his line of vision, she dropped it comfortably into the pocket of her jeans.

Old Cars, Young Towers

EMILY came home to an empty house one afternoon at the beginning of the summer holidays. Jo had gone swimming with Lydia; Roland was probably in the garage, painting his bike for about the sixteenth time, changing its colour from purple to a loud orange in preparation for his week's camping with Clive; Aunt Deb was just about due back from a shopping expedition to London. As Emily came to the house she saw a man standing at the door. She recognised Tad Fletcher, the works manager Jo so heartily disliked, and whose trouble-making potentialities had worried both Gilbert and David Tower. Tad had been over a year at the works now, and there had been no trouble of any kind—except for the Kojo incident, which had certainly not been anything to do with union matters.

Emily said 'Hullo', and Tad Fletcher turned and grinned at her and said 'Hullo' back.

'I was hoping to see Mr David,' he said, still using the old manner of address, though in fact David was now the only real Tower with the firm. 'There doesn't seem to be anyone at home.'

'Aunt Deb's been to London. She'll be back any minute, I should think. I expect Uncle David's gone to meet her train. Will you come in and wait?'

'All right. I don't mind. I shan't keep him long, anyway, but I'd better see him.'

'Nothing wrong at the works, I hope?' said Emily conversationally, as she showed him in.

He laughed. She wondered why Jo disliked him, for he had a good firm face with a lot of creases. 'Now you don't expect me to discuss works business with you, do you?'

'Not if you don't want to, of course. Sorry. We always ask Uncle David when he comes in—has he had a good day—that sort of thing. Still—sorry. I expect you thought I was prying.'

'I never know what to think about any one of you lot, and that's a fact,' he admitted. 'I'm glad all my kids seem fairly easy. At least—I think I'm glad.'

'How many kids have you got, then?'

'Three. Ken—he's sixteen; Roger, twelve; Janet, nine.'

'Will the boys go into the works?'

'Ken will. He'll be at the Tech. next term, along with some of you.'

'Oliver will be starting then,' said Emily, 'and Kojo.'

'Kojo? He's one of you, is he?'

'Oh yes, he is,' said Emily firmly.

'He hasn't had much of a time of it at the works.'

'It's been all right since that time—you know. Hasn't it?' she asked, frowning suddenly. She wanted Kojo to be happy because it was on her account that he had been brought here. But somewhere at the back of her mind was the niggling thought that he might not be as settled and content as she always told him he was.

'I don't think it's been that easy,' Tad said. 'I never thought it would be, myself.'

Emily remembered, then, why it was that Jo disliked Tad. It was because he had once said that all he asked of labour was that it should be *white, keen and qualified*. She looked at his decent, rather humorous face, and saw that besides the humour there was purpose, strength and stubbornness. Whatever differences one might have had with Tad Fletcher they would not be insignificant ones.

At this point Jo came bounding into the house with Lydia in tow.

'Decided not to swim—too jolly chilly.' Then she saw the visitor and checked slightly, 'Hullo, Tad,' she said casually.

'Hullo, Jo,' he replied, in precisely the same tone. And they looked at one another stiffly, measuring up. Then they both relaxed and started to laugh in the same instant. 'I came to see your dad,' he decided to explain. He nodded amiably at Lydia who had now come up to the group and was standing looking a bit prim.

'He's been telling me about his children while he waits,' Emily said to Jo.

'I didn't know he'd got any.'

'Oh yes—he's quite a human being, actually,' said Tad. 'Eats, walks and sleeps like any real man.'

'Oh lor'.' Jo was reddening now. 'Don't let me get away with anything, will you?' Then they were laughing again, and almost friends.

'Here they are,' said Lydia, in a rather relieved tone, as the car drew up outside. Roland was a few paces behind on his bike, and he wheeled it sharply round the car making piercing siren noises.

Deborah Tower came into the house looking as pleased to be home as if she had been away for a year. The girls threw themselves at her—at least, Emily did, and Lydia did, while Jo made noises in the background. David took Tad Fletcher off to his study.

'Did you see Uncle Saville?' Jo asked her mother.

'I had lunch with him.'

'Did you? Or did he have lunch with you?'

'Well, I invited him,' her mother replied rather defensively. 'You watch out, Jo—you're getting as stuffy about poor Saville as all the rest of the Towers. Yes, I know,' she said quickly, as Jo laughed, 'I can be pretty stuffy about poor Saville myself. But he's *such* good company. He sent you his love.'

'He must have known we'd been talking about him,' Jo said. 'Emily and I were making up a story about the old cars, and how we bought them, and then bought the Cross Street chapel to keep them in, and then paid Uncle Saville a handsome salary to be curator of the Tower Transport Museum . . .'

'It was a good story while it lasted,' said Emily.

Lydia stood looking primmer than ever—not at all like her usual self. She had a blind spot when it came to Jo's Uncle Saville. She still felt convinced that if he had hung on to his few shares in Tower Motors, instead of taking the profit on a sale, the take-over would have been miraculously held up. She, too, had been thinking about the cars, for Clive spoke perpetually of the disaster of losing them. Because she had been planning her stables, she had become aware of the extraordinary jumble of outbuildings at Eason Elms, and the enormous amount of space lying idle.

'If we could only get hold of the actual cars,' she said now, 'I believe nearly all of them would fit into the big barn.'

'But you can't get hold of them,' Deborah said, 'and you all of you know you can't. So do for goodness' sake stop moaning about it. It's a horrible thing to have happened—I know that just as well as you do—but there's nothing to be done about it now . . . Here —I bought you these sweaters in the sales. Lydia—Emily—Jo. I hope I've got you the right size, Lydia.'

While they were dealing with this distraction, the two men came out of the study and David went with Tad Fletcher to the door. 'We'll keep our fingers crossed, then,' they heard David say. Then he shut the door and came across to the sitting-room, where they were strewing paper over the floor as Deborah undid her purchases.

'What did he want?' Jo asked.

'Ho hum,' said David, 'never a smell of labour trouble while Tower Motors was Tower Motors. Now here they are threatening a walk-out.'

'Oh whatever *for*?' cried Deborah.

'Something to do with working conditions.'

'What's that mean precisely?'

'Well, I can't help laughing, as they say,' said David, looking particularly unamused. 'Working conditions have always suited our chaps all right. C.M.H. have imported twenty or thirty workers—and nothing's good enough for them. They're kicking up one hell of a shindy because the canteen's crowded and there are too few lavatories. Obviously twenty-odd extra just tip the scales. I can't see C.M.H. running up a new block overnight, so presumably the labour force must be scaled down again. That'll mean putting out the local men—not the new lot. The old hands will be the ones to go ... Oh well—perhaps my life's been too easy and I need shaking up.'

Lydia said she had better go home now, and Jo went with her to the door. They always had a lot to talk about, so from the door Jo walked to the gate, and then out as far as the corner of the lane.

'Did you mean it about the cars, Lydia? Would there be room?'

'The barn's colossal. Clive thinks it's almost as big as the shed at the works. I expect we should do some measuring.'

'I expect we should do some thinking about money,' replied Jo. 'We'd have to buy the cars back, I suppose. How could we?'

'Clive said if you borrowed money to buy the cars, then you could sell about five and have enough to pay off most of the debt.'

'It can't be as easy as that. He must be a financial wizard, though, mustn't he? Fancy thinking of it. Clever. And you're clever, too, Lydia, to have had the idea about the barn. I don't expect you to bother much about the cars.'

'It's all very well to be clever,' said Lydia, accepting the compliment with modest pleasure, 'but it would be better to be rich. Perhaps Auntie Jay could lend the money? Or Anthea's in-laws —they seem to be rolling.'

'*Something* might happen,' Jo decided. 'I shall go down and measure up. I'll go on Sunday. I can get in through the old gap down by the scrap yard. The rest's easy. I've still got the key.'

Jo's immediate instinct was to get hold of Oliver so that they could break into the works together. Then she changed her mind and decided to go alone. It was a slightly mad enterprise, so the fewer people involved, the better. It seemed a long time till Sunday, with a Saturday morning in between on which no single one of them attempted to visit the works. They kept out of one another's way, too. The situation was too painful even for discussion.

Discussion of one kind or another was going on all the time. Would there be a walk-out? Would it lead to a fully-fledged strike? Jo felt that the place had become a battlefield for a kind of civil war, and as she went down quietly towards the works on Sunday morning, she felt like a resistance worker, like a woman fighter of the underground bearing weapons to the beleaguered. She grew increasingly free in her imaginings, and began to believe that she might find the members of the old guard, the employees for years of Tower Motors, barricaded inside the building, with thermos flasks and packets of sandwiches, bottles of beer and hard-boiled eggs and tomatoes—the last more probably to hurl than to eat.

The scrap yard was a horrible area at the back of the works, on the banks of the small scummy canal that tied the loop of the river into a ring, for what original benefit it was now hard to understand. Every now and again there would be a clearance in the yard, and an enormous holocaust of old tyres, upholstered seats, torn hoods and various other paraphernalia attaching to dead motor cars. In the past, this unpleasant spot had been a hunting ground for young Towers in search of materials for one project or another. It was a long time since Jo had been near the place and it was even danker and sourer than she remembered. Old batteries lay in a huge mound, oil cans and petrol cans were everywhere, and there was the terrible skeleton of a sports car that had been fired, either in an attempt to dispose of the wreckage or as the result of an accident, there was no telling which. Grass of a hairy sort sprouted in tufts among coils of rusty wire; and there was a positive thicket of stunted elder trees growing in a compost of sodden cardboard boxes, old string, dreadful wads of cotton cleaning waste and rags that looked as though they had once been somebody's winter combinations.

The entrance to this paradise was through a gap wrenched conveniently in the iron railing that surrounded the yard on two sides. There was a well-worn path on both sides of the gap, for not only Tower children had found the place useful. Approaching the gap, Jo had wondered if she would still be able to squeeze through, but it was easy. A swan on the stagnant canal watched her, hissed at her when she spoke kindly, and shook its behind contemptuously before gliding away.

Because it was Sunday, because the place was deserted, because of the still sunny morning and the disembodied sound of radios playing an unattended church service from the cottages that bordered the nearby river, Jo felt as though she might be the last person alive in the whole world. She knew now that there were no entrenched workers and that she was no heroine; that this sneaking into a place where she was no longer welcome had about it something squalid and humiliating. For a second or two she considered turning on her heel and making for home, but the key burnt a hole in her pocket, where lay also the notebook and pencil with which she proposed to reduce the Tower collection of veteran cars to a manageable inventory. It was as though by doing this she would somehow reclaim what was lost.

Somewhere about the building there would be a watchman. He might be in the cubby-hole at the gates, but he was more probably, this being Sunday, snug in the office in the main hall. Approaching from the scrap yard, Jo had no need to pass either danger point. She picked her way carefully and quietly. She was frightened while she was fitting the key and opening the door, but the instant she was inside the shed she felt easy. She closed the door behind her, got out her measure and her notebook and set to. No one interrupted her. No sound made her jump. The sun shone beyond the high windows, the cars stood waiting for whatever fate was in store. Measuring them and noting their contents, a loving but largely superfluous exercise, took a very long time. By half past twelve, when she had planned to leave, she was no more than a quarter of the way round. The David Towers were going to lunch with the Brian Millers and she would be terribly late by the time she had got home and changed. She did then what she could just as easily have done in the first place—she paced out the dimensions of the shed to compare with those of the Holts' barn at Eason Elms.

When that was done, Jo let herself out as carefully and discreetly as she had come in. As she crossed the open space in front of the shed, moving in the direction of the scrap yard, a man appeared walking towards the shed she had just left.

Jo had the immediate, ostrich-like conviction that so long as she didn't look at him he would be unable to see her. She went straight on, nearly suffocated by the shocked banging of her heart. He called out—shouted after her. For a split second she was lifting her feet to run, but they were as heavy as feet in a dream and she had no breath left anyway. So she turned.

'Yes?' she said, as insolently as she could.

Instead of the watchman she had expected—an old friend, he might very well have been—she found herself face to face with James Halliday, the new boss, C.M.H.'s man who had replaced Robert Tower in the control and management of the organisation.

Jo said, 'Good morning, Mr Halliday.' He did not answer, so she added, 'I know you from your photograph in the *Echo*.' Still he said nothing. 'It was a bad photograph,' Jo persevered. 'I think you're better looking.' The words, pert and horrible in her ears, burst out from sheer despair.

When he spoke at last he said she had the advantage of him. He had not seen her photograph in the *Echo*. He was tall, thin, greyish, confident—and not particularly unfriendly. But his *Who are you?* stance was intimidating.

'I'm Jo Tower,' she said.

'Oh, so that's it. David Tower's girl, aren't you? I did rather wonder—there's a likeness, of course.' And as though she had really explained practically everything now, he went on, 'You might be just the person I need. I came in this morning specially to look at the old cars in the shed here. I'm told they're very fine. My first chance to look them over. You could show me round.'

Jo slunk towards the shed like a fugitive turned back at the frontier. They both paused at the door. There was a tussle of wills, for she waited to see him bring out his key, while he, knowing perfectly well that she had one herself, waited for her. He was bound to win. Jo was almost whimpering as she unlocked the door, and it was worse then, for he held out his hand and she was obliged to give him the key, which after all was not really hers to keep. A nice mess she had made of things now.

'I think I ought to go,' she said. 'I'm going to be dreadfully late for lunch. We're going to the Millers—my uncle Brian Miller —you know . . .'

'Before you run away,' he said, 'if you really must—and I would have appreciated a guided tour—let me say something. You can always come in here when you want to—there's no need to sneak in like a thief. Not into the repair shop, nowhere in the works, please—I've heard all about that and the general foreman knows now that I won't have it at any price. But no one can object to your coming in here.' He waited for her to thank him, but she couldn't; she was hearing his words about the repair shop ringing and ringing in her ears. 'Make the most of it, I should,' he said, sounding—and understandably—slightly annoyed at her lack of reaction. 'They won't be here very long, I fancy.'

That stung her. 'Why not?'

'The powers that be are talking of selling. We need the space. I'm afraid one can't be sentimental about it. Lovely old cars, of course, but we're not dealing every day in lovely old cars, are we? There've been several offers, I understand. Some are vintage, aren't they?'

'Six of them.'

'Wasn't there some fair or fête or something last summer—where they were driven in procession?'

'At Milsom Magnificorum,' she said faintly.

'That's it. I remember seeing an account—there was quite good press coverage. You know what enthusiasts are, they always manage to hear about their special interests. Then they swoop like vultures when there's any chance of a sale.'

Moment by moment, things were getting worse. It had been her idea to use the cars in the procession at the festival. Uncle Saville had actually brought things to a head, but she was the one who had persuaded Uncle Robert. And she was always held responsible for Uncle Saville's doings, anyway.

'Who wants them?' she asked.

'I couldn't tell you that even if I wanted to. It's the business of Head Office. A couple of offers from America, I believe—maybe more than that. And a French gentleman has staked a claim to the Rolls, if the collection is to be broken up.'

Jo turned and started walking away, but he caught her up. 'It's just the way of things, my dear,' he said, brisk but quite kind. 'Now, cheer up. I shall hang the key up in the office and you can always ask for it. I'll see it's all right. Now—why don't I run you home since you say you're so late?'

'I've got my bike ... Thanks awfully ...' She was moving off again, but she had to turn back because she remembered that the bicycle was standing against the railings on the far side of the scrap yard. She made a humiliating retreat, and he watched her all the way—or so she believed.

Lunch with the Millers that Sunday was a very crowded function. With Paul and Anthea and the baby still staying there the house was crammed at the outset. The David Towers added six to the original number, for Kojo was included in the invitation. Margaret had also invited Adwoa. However, Hugh and Robin were off on some ploy of their own, which took away two from the expected total.

It was fine enough to eat in the garden. Margaret had arranged all the food in the kitchen, and they were to help themselves and then move outside.

The Millers were the only branch of the family to live in a modern house with lots of big clear windows, unpolished pale wood and bright curtains. When Brian Miller married Patricia Tower they went to live in a converted farmhouse on the outskirts of the town. Anthea and the twins had grown up there, and Sukey had been twelve when they left. When Patricia died and Margaret came to look after them all, Brian sold up and moved to a house as different as possible from that first one. So this present house had really always been Margaret's, and it was stamped from the outset with her personality. The kitchen, as Jo said to Sukey while they piled up their plates, was downright dreamy.

Jo had changed in a rush, longing to talk to Oliver or Lydia rather than be sociable with the Millers. But now she was grateful for the distraction offered by a fair-sized party. Anyway, she had been able immediately on arrival to pour out the story of the morning to Anthea and Paul, which had at least unburdened her conscience a little.

Jo and Sukey took their plates out into the garden. It had nothing but mown grass and trees, and the effect was lovely—cool and smooth, shady and sunny in all the right places. Emily sat on the ground with Adwoa and Kojo and they talked together in another language, all three getting highly excited and laughing loudly together, so that the rest felt they should be left alone. At a safe distance, like spectators at a fair, Penny and Rachel stood watching and listening, the food threatening to slide off their plates as they became increasingly absorbed.

'Rose would be furious,' Sukey muttered to Jo, flicking a glance at Kojo and Adwoa. 'Oh wouldn't she just!'

'Where is she? I haven't seen her for ages.' The last time, Jo recalled, Rose had been furious, too.

'I hope she's far away, Jo. Oh I hope she's very far away!'

But when they had finished their lunch and Margaret had made coffee in vast quantities, Hugh and Robin turned up, with one strange girl, called Julie something—and Rose.

'I know I wasn't invited, darling,' Rose said, as she kissed the air on either side of Margaret's face, 'but I did so want to see something more of Anthea. I know she won't be here much longer.'

'Well, of course—and it's lovely to see you,' Margaret replied. 'Your mother told me you were all going to the Etheringtons for the weekend.'

'They've gone,' said Rose. 'What a lot of people. Do I know everybody?'

'It's only family,' Margaret assured her.

At this moment Adwoa came into the house with a pile of plates, calling as she came, 'Who will help me wash the dishes, please?' Then she saw Rose and said without a pause, 'Ah—you have come in time to work!'

'I've come in time to avoid it,' said Rose. 'Why not ask Kojo to help you?'

There was no more than a second's pause, yet it was time enough to hear a sound as of small swords clashing together. Then Adwoa laughed and said there were plenty of girls, so surely they could do it?

'Back to the kitchen, eh?' Rose said. 'What a savage attitude.' As she spoke she turned on her heel and walked towards the garden, pushing past Emily who was standing holding a tray of glasses, stunned by what she had heard. 'Wake up,' said Rose, 'and let your elders by.'

Adwoa went straight on into the kitchen. 'I'll do the washing,' she said. 'Will you dry, Emily?'

'We'll all help,' Jo cried, snatching at cloths. 'Here, Emily— catch. One for you, Sukey . . . No—three to dry and one to wash won't do. You'd better put-away, Sukey, otherwise Adwoa will never keep up with us.'

Adwoa was quiet for a minute or two, then she joined easily enough in the chatter that the others had kept up rather desperately. The tension was smoothed away. The crisis seemed to be past.

The enormous pile of washing-up was only half dealt with when Kojo appeared in the kitchen doorway. He ignored the rest and spoke directly to Adwoa in his own language.

Emily said sharply, 'No, Kojo! You don't mean that!'

Kojo did not answer her or look at her, but spoke again to Adwoa. She hesitated, looking from him to Emily and back again. Then without a word to anyone, she took off her borrowed apron, hung it over a chair, and followed Kojo out of the room. It was all so swift and smooth that the others had barely a chance to understand what was happening.

'What did he say, Emily?' Jo asked.

'I don't want to tell you.'

'You must.'

'He said: "Come away with me from this accursed place. I will care for you."'

'He didn't really mean it? He couldn't!'

'He meant it when he said it,' Emily replied soberly.

Jo burst out, 'That blasted Rose! Why don't I go and tear her hair out by the handful? That'd show her which of us are savages!'

Sukey ran to the window. 'They're going! They're going!'

'What ought we to do, Emily?' Jo asked. 'We ought to go after them. You go—you can talk to them and we can't.'

'I expect he'll just take her home ... We can't do anything. He won't come back now.' It was a long time since they had seen Emily looking so unhappy.

Out in the garden Rose was playing loudly and wildly with the two little girls. The parents, talking seriously together in the sitting-room, about the works, the possible walk-out, the whole wretched situation, were entirely ignorant of trouble nearer home. In blissful ignorance, too, Anthea and Paul were walking under the trees at the bottom of the garden, taking it in turns to carry the baby. Hugh joined Rose and his young sisters, perhaps in some desire to quiet things down, but Roland stirred them up again by joining in, too. The noise was considerable. Only Robin and the strange girl called Julie-something were quiet, sitting on a bench by the magnolia tree, each entirely occupied with the silent study of the other's face.

'I thought Robin had some Austrian girl in tow,' Jo said.

'No, that was Hugh,' Sukey muttered, watching from the kitchen window. 'Oh isn't he disgusting? He looks as though he could eat her but he'll be vile about her when she's gone.'

It was no good trying to work up a rival interest to Kojo and Adwoa. The unhappy drama of their exit hung over the bright kitchen, the pleasant sunny day, the family councils that seemed twice as important now as they had ever been. It was almost a relief when the party broke up.

'We've been making plans, Emily,' Anthea told her, as the David Towers were leaving. 'Aunt Deb says your American aunt is wailing for you. You could travel over with us, if you liked.'

'It would be a good way to do what I don't want to do,' Emily agreed.

'She's afraid Aunt Sam may lock her up and keep her for ever,' Roland said.

'Oh I'm not, Roland! I'm not quite such an idiot. It won't seem so far if I can go with Anthea and Paul.'

'And we could always come and *un*lock you, couldn't we?' Paul suggested.

'It's the best possible idea,' Deborah said. 'Your aunt will know you must be back for the beginning of the autumn term, Emily.'

Emily nodded. What she wanted most was to fly to Ghana, to see Amma, and her parents and the new baby, to see Africa again and know that there had once been a younger Emily with different eyes and different thoughts—yet not a different Emily. If she could only connect her present self with that younger girl, left behind like a corpse, like a ghost after the tragedy of her parents' death—

so many things might fall into place. She would see the future then, not in any fantastic or debatable way but as it was, in colour and perspective, bit by bit . . .

When they got back there was no sign of Kojo. The excuse they had given the grown-ups, that he had taken Adwoa home, had anyway seemed thin, for it meant that neither had had the manners to say goodbye to Margaret and Brian. So now the whole wretched tale had to come out. Though not, certainly, what more Rose had said to make Kojo come stalking into the house—Emily was thankful no one seemed to have heard that, whatever it might have been.

'I can't understand Rose,' Deborah Tower cried. 'I simply can't begin to understand her. She has no business to turn the boy's head in this way.'

'Why should she turn his head?' Emily asked, in a rather thin voice.

'Because he *is* only a boy. He must be nearly two years younger than she is.'

'That wasn't what you meant.'

'No. Well. All right, Emily—I suppose I meant the colour thing. I'm sorry—I should know better. But Rose is a very attractive girl and he was bound to be flattered by so much notice.'

'Kojo thinks Adwoa is ten times prettier than Rose. Why shouldn't he? You don't think Kojo's better looking than Hugh or Roland or Oliver. Why should Kojo think Rose is prettier than Adwoa? Some white people are absolutely hideous. I got quite a shock when I saw a lot of them together for the first time.'

'Oh do be quiet, Emily. It's easy to be righteous. We should all be able to behave much better than we do, all of us. We've all got stupid and self-conscious about this business. However, I don't really expect to be taken to task by a girl of your age. Let's leave it at that.'

Jo and Roland looked at their mother soberly. She did not often lose her calm. The fact that she had done so with Emily set the seal on the fact that she now had a family of three children and was prepared to treat them equally. She had never rebuked Emily before and she was probably as surprised as any of them. She left the room at once.

'Oh damn it,' said Emily, so flatly that Roland half laughed.

Jo gave a huffing sigh and threw herself into a chair. 'What a day!' She had not had a chance yet to tell anyone but Anthea and Paul about Mr Halliday, and how the old cars were probably to be sold.

'I didn't mean to make her cross, Jo.'

'No, I'm sure you didn't. You just sounded so horribly smug.'

'I didn't mean to.'

'I know you didn't mean to. She didn't mean to snap, either, I daresay.'

'You all think you're so decent to treat Kojo as an equal, but you know very well you don't *think* he's equal.'

That bit deep, and Jo said flatly, 'Any minute now I'll wring your pretty little neck.'

'She won't really,' Roland told Emily.

He sounded so earnest and reassuring that Jo leapt up and rushed from the room before the whole dramatic scene collapsed in screams of laughter. She would telephone Oliver and tell him the long tale of the day's doings. No—she would telephone Lydia first, because she had been so decent to think of the barn.

However, the bell rang before Jo could pick up the receiver and dial her number. Perhaps it was Kojo. She sounded a bit breathless as she answered.

A boy's voice spoke to her, but nor Kojo's. Nor any that she knew immediately.

'It's Chris,' he said. 'Remember?'

'Chris . . . ? Oh—you mean Chris and Ron?'

'Don't go muddling us up. I'm the handsome one with the nice ways.'

'You're the tall one,' she corrected him.

'Tall, handsome and kind-hearted. Look—your chum. The one from Ghana—'

'Kojo.'

'That's him. Joko, more like. See if you can stop him coming to the works on Monday.'

'Why?'

'Just stop him, there's a good girl.'

'*Why?*'

'Trouble,' he said. And hung up.

10

Oliver

IT was not possible to do a single thing about Chris's warning, for the very simple reason that Kojo did not return home that night, nor did he telephone. It seemed most likely that he was still with Adwoa—one of her three flat-mates was on holiday, so there would be a room for him there. Unfortunately the flat had no telephone. The anxiety David and Deborah Tower felt about Kojo rather overwhelmed the development hinted at by Chris— in a way Jo had the feeling that her father was glad of an opportunity to dismiss that altogether. In this crisis, everyone turned to Emily as being the one most likely to know how Kojo might behave.

'Perhaps he will go home.'

'Home? Do you mean right home? To Ghana?'

'Yes, I do.'

'But that would be dreadful—a complete proof of failure—of our failure,' David Tower cried.

'Or perhaps he will feel calmer tomorrow,' Emily suggested quickly, hating his distress. They had helped Kojo to England for her sake and this was the result. Why had she supposed it would be otherwise? Kojo had no ties with England and he could just as well have been trained as a technician in his own country. The whole business, she saw now, had been a terrible mistake. Away from his own environment, he had not even been the Kojo she remembered with so much affection. He had been pinched and shy and solemn and his attempts at friendliness and enthusiasm were those of a person quite different from the easy, intelligent boy she had known. In her heart she had known he was homesick, and because she had not wanted to know how much, she had been no help to him. No wonder he had accepted Rose's friendship and then suffered for it. Unlike the more buoyant Adwoa, his temperament had found the change of setting and values too difficult.

Waking on Monday morning, after a miserable night, Emily could not imagine what any one of them ought to do next. She felt heavy-headed, feverish—she knew these signs but did not want to admit them. They were part of what Jo had called her 'third eye', and Emily had accepted that that eye was now closed permanently. Besides, these symptoms could as well be nothing more sinister than the result of a disturbed night. One of the conflicts which had occupied Emily a great deal recently was the fact that her premonitions, or previsions, or whatever anyone liked to call them, could just as well be quite baseless, a lot of nonsense built on that one remark of Mrs Amponsah's, made long ago about a *terrible gift*. Certainly at the picnic at Thrumble Rows that first summer in England she had experienced a dreadful oppression—but a great many others might have felt the same, given the particular circumstances. Then there had been her fears at the festival at Milsom Magnificorum, her certainty that one of the cars in the rally would crash—and the fact that this might indeed have happened. But again—hadn't she put two and two together to make a very questionable five? Couldn't it have been simply that her parents' death in a car crash had made her hyper-sensitive about driving in general—particularly in the conditions following torrential rain?

Emily lay in bed puzzling about her own imagination, and about what she could possibly do to help in this emergency. Should she get up now and go down to the works, hoping that Kojo might turn up? Or wait, hoping instead that he would not leave England without telling her that he was going? She remembered what Jo had told her of Chris's warning. She also remembered Tad Fletcher and what he had said about *white, keen and qualified.* Although her Uncle David insisted that there was no prejudice, no colour bar in Milsom Parva or at the works, it had to be remembered that a body of workers from C.M.H. in the Midlands had been injected into the local works—to increase productivity it was said. They, after all, were the ones discontented with working conditions. Was the over-crowded canteen of their complaints overcrowded in a particular way that they objected to? Overcrowded with African Kojo, in fact?'

It was half-past six on a fine summer morning. The first shift went on at 7.30, while David Tower arrived at his office shortly after nine. There would be plenty of time for Emily to cycle to the works and get back for breakfast before anyone missed her. She slid out of bed and set about dressing. She heard someone go downstairs and told herself Aunt Deb was on her way to make a pot of tea—she was a great one for tea in the early morning and no doubt she, too, had slept badly. As soon as she had returned upstairs and shut the bedroom door, Emily slipped out.

Now that she was on her feet, the feeling of strain increased. She fetched her bicycle more or less at the double, wheeled it along the grass for the sake of silence, and set off, up the hill from the river, then steeply down again to its eastward curve, the early sun in her eyes. As she went she was still fighting with her feelings of coming trouble, trying to rationalise yet again the past experiences which had seemed so mysterious at the time. And again the three occasions buzzed in her mind—the fatal crash that had orphaned her: Thrumble Rows; the festival rally . . . As that last occasion forced itself into the forefront of her mind, Emily was dazzlingly sure that something about that day was continuing—that something avoided then still threatened. At this point she was almost certain that her deepest distress was not to do with Kojo

at all. Her impulse was almost to abandon him to his fate and concentrate on what really mattered. But what was that? A great
many people had been concerned with that other occasion, whose
image seemed now to be bouncing back at her, as though the
past were a satellite receiving and transmitting messages. Who, of
them all, did she feel the need to protect or to warn?

Emily both resented and suspected her own intuitions—there
could be some kind of devil pulling her in a false direction. She
continued towards the works.

There were a lot of men about when Emily warily approached
the works and pushed her bike against a shop front opposite, so
that she could watch what went on without drawing attention to
herself. The men seemed to be going in through the gates, talking
briefly and then coming out again. There was no sign of Kojo. He
was always impeccably punctual so she was convinced he was not
coming. She could return home with that particular problem
settled.

'Good morning to you,' a man said, as she pushed past a parked
car. It was Tad Fletcher, 'You're early about. Come to study
industrial relations, have you?'

'Not precisely,' said Emily, very precisely indeed. 'Is it a strike?'

'Technically a walk-out. Any minute now it'll be unofficially
a strike. That means it's not my strike, not by any means. Still—I
can see their point. You know what I always say?'

'I only know one thing you said once—about *white, keen and
qualified.*'

'Out of the mouths, eh?' said Tad, laughing and making a
grimace of surprise. 'You're a Tower in the making, all right.
You get on home now, there's a good lass. I'll take my oath you've
had no breakfast yet.'

'Is *white* a part of it?'

'White is a part of it.'

'You didn't tell Uncle David that.'

'If you'll forgive me saying so, there's none so deaf as them that
won't hear. But you listen, lass—you listen. Your dark young

friend hasn't turned up, I see. Tell him to stay away. Do that for
both of us.'

'I'll do it for him,' said Emily.

'Okay, Miss Tower,' Tad said grinning. 'Do it for all of us.'

The morning was difficult. Kojo did not appear. David Tower
was in conference with the management from half past nine
onwards. Deborah said she would drive the fifteen miles or so to
Adwoa's flat to see if she could find out anything.

'You'd better come with me, Emily.'

But they drew a blank. The flat was silent. No one at all was
there.

In the afternoon there was still no news, though Deborah had
finally and reluctantly telephoned the Cardews' house to see if
Rose could tell her anything. But Rose was occupied with her
own private humiliations.

'I suppose he's with that wretched girl,' she said.

'I hope so,' replied Deborah coldly. She hung up and said to
Jo, who was standing near, 'What are we going to do now? I've
got a hospital committee meeting at three and I really think I
must go to it. I suppose life can't come entirely to a standstill
because of all this.'

'I'll be here,' Jo said. 'And Emily. And Oliver said he'd be over.
We've got things to discuss.' She meant the old cars, but she
wouldn't say so because her mother had become so impatient of
this hopeless preoccupation.

In fact Clive as well as Oliver turned up that afternoon. His
holiday had begun. Jo's encounter with Mr Halliday had passed
pretty quickly into family coinage and everyone knew about it
by now.

Emily let Clive in. 'How's the Morris?' she asked, for she was
growing knowledgable.

'All right. Why shouldn't she be?' Clive was as touchy as the
parent of a delinquent child.

'You did say something about the big end,' she reminded him.

'I've said something about everything at one time or another—from the steering to the water pump. But she's just been passed fit. Don't you start telling me I ought to get rid of her.'

'All right, I won't,' said Emily, thinking that it was Clive's car she had fussed about on the day of the festival rally, and here it was still in condition.

'There is a bit of a knocking,' he admitted, giving in suddenly. 'I think it's just a body noise, but I'll run Jo round and get her to listen. She's got a better ear than any of us.'

Jo was delighted with the distraction and said they should take time to go out to the airfield where both she and Oliver would be able to drive on the weed-grown runways without breaking any laws.

'You come, too, Emily,' she suggested.

'No, I'll stay. Suppose Kojo came and the house was empty?'

'Are you sure you don't mind?' Jo insisted, looking rather guilty. 'He could always wait, couldn't he? We shan't be too long.'

'I'd rather stay.'

So they went off and left her. No more than ten minutes after the Morris had vanished, Kojo walked in.

He said at once, 'Where is Mrs Tower?'

'Out. Where have you been?' Seeing him perfectly well and normal, her anger rose.

'In London,' he replied.

'In London? Whatever for? We thought you must be with Adwoa.'

'Adwoa was with me,' he corrected her. 'We have been at the Embassy seeing about tickets and passports and such things. You know.'

'Passports . . . Not Adwoa, too?'

'We shall leave tomorrow. She was to go home soon anyway.'

'Where is she, then?'

'In London. With a friend from the hospital—where she trained. We went there from the railway station last night. Adwoa telephoned and at once this lady said, "Come". She is very kind. Helpful.'

'You make it sound as though she's the only one who's kind and helpful.'

'No. I do not mean that at all.'

'You're running away,' said Emily.

'Perhaps I am running away, yes. But I must go, Emily. Let me go. I came to England to see you. I wanted to make many friends. But in the end I have only one besides you, and she is my own sort. I think this is sad.' He looked at her and frowned. 'I have tried to be happy here,' he said. 'Believe me, Emily, I have tried.'

'Oh Kojo—must you go? Must you? When you get back and think about us all—we shan't seem so bad . . .'

'It is nothing that you would do. But there is too much besides.'

'I wish I could come with you, then. Just for a time. To see Amma and your father and your mother. And Yao. And the new little sister.'

'You will come,' he said, and now he smiled at her. 'But it will not be for ever. Once, it might have been. But not now. Is that right?'

She nodded. Both knew where her home was.

'I came back to say goodbye and to get my things. Please help me to pack them, Emily. And then I must go to the works.'

They were on their way upstairs and she stopped dead. Is it this? she wondered. Is it Kojo after all . . . ? 'Why?' she asked.

'Well, I am short of money because I did a stupid thing. On Friday there was some unpleasantness—'

'What unpleasantness?'

'It's over and it was nothing. But I left quickly. I left my overalls and my week's pay in the pocket. I must go to fetch it.'

'You won't get in. There's a strike or something. Stay till Aunt Deb gets back and she'll lend you some money.'

'But when will that be? I have to catch the London train.'

She was stuffing his clothes into the big leather hold-all. 'Then I'll go and fetch the money,' she said.

'They won't give it to you.'

They went on packing.

'This is an awful weight, Kojo. You'll need a taxi.' If she could delay him long enough the others would come back—they could not be very long, surely?

'I wish I could have seen Mrs Tower. Please explain to her.'

'There are men outside the gates—sure to be. Pickets, aren't they? I'm sure Oliver said so once.'

'Goodbye, Emily. I must go now.'

'Pickets,' she repeated. 'To stop people getting in. To stop everybody—anybody. But most of all Kojo.'

'I know what you are telling me,' he cried, suddenly bursting out wildly. 'Isn't it enough that I have been called a black savage by your beautiful cousin Rose—that Adwoa has been insulted? Must you tell me that I have brought trouble on all your family by causing this worry at the works? Must you make me understand this?' He seized the hold-all and swung to the head of the stairs. 'Goodbye, Emily. I am sorry I have shouted. I must go now.'

She ran down the stairs after him. 'Stop, Kojo! Wait!'

'That's enough now,' he said, pushing her away because she had grabbed his arm. Then he was through the door and out into the drive. He went round the back way, taking the short cut across the garden that he had learnt to use in the months he had been with them.

Emily began to shiver. She hated her failure to persuade him. She ran to the telephone, found the works number and dialled. The bell rang and rang, but she hung on, convinced someone must answer. And after a long time there was a great clatter as a hand grabbed the receiver, and a big rough voice answered the call. Emily asked to speak to Mr David Tower.

'No one here,' said the man. And hung up.

Emily had to start waiting again—for the sound of Aunt Deb;

for the sound of the Morris; for the voices of Clive and Jo and Oliver. So long as the car was really in working order, so long as Jo had not listened and suggested some immediately dangerous flaw, they would have to turn straight round and drive to the works to head Kojo off. It was quite a walk. There would be time if only they returned soon.

They had dallied on the air strip because it was such a gorgeous opportunity, as Jo said, for behaving like maniacs. There was not a soul to be seen. The bleached grass and the humps of camomile bursting through the battered concrete, the broken-down hangars that once had sheltered aeroplanes that had seemed giants, shimmered in the hazy hot afternoon. How small and sad it all looked, if you measured it by its past. How absolutely magnificent it seemed to young Towers with the knowledge but not the authority to drive and drive fairly fast. Clive, who was a model of decency when he was on the road, went round the track like a Grand Prix driver. Oliver, when he took his turn, had less dash but more style. Jo tried hard for both. The dear old Morris snorted like a cavalry charger, but she could not give them much more than sixty or so at her age.

'One more lap, and then home,' Clive decided. 'Make the most of it—five more minutes and we've got to behave decently.'

He went round the course singing at the top of his voice. Jo and Oliver sat in the back, not on the seats, but on the folded hood. It was a bumpy ride that way and they both nearly overbalanced at the start. Then they locked their arms round one another for steadiness, leaning like motor cyclists against the curves that Clive cut fine on this last circuit. At the end they both slid down into the back seat, breathless and wind-blown and shaken with laughter.

'*Summer ti-ime* . . .' Jo sang, her eyes closed, a wide blissful smile on her face, '*tum-te tum-te, tum tum tum* . . .' Then she opened her eyes and saw Oliver grinning back at her. For a second she seemed to hang suspended in time, in a moment that took her back to that other moment when she had seemed to say too much too soon. Only this time she forgot to be embarrassed as she had been then. They looked at one another in what she thought of afterwards as a recognising way ... Then Clive spoke to Oliver and it was over and they were on their way home.

Emily was at the gate watching for them.

'Now what?' said Jo. 'We oughtn't to have stayed away so long. We oughtn't to have enjoyed ourselves like that. Oh lor'—something's happened!'

Oliver shouted to Emily—'What's up?'

'Is the car all right?' Emily called.

'Poifect, as far as Our Expert can tell,' Clive answered.

'Then, please, Clive, turn it round and go down to the works. Kojo's been here. He's leaving for Ghana tomorrow and Adwoa's going with him and He's gone to collect his pay packet—he left it behind on Friday. Please stop him. You'll catch him if you're quick.'

'Pickets,' said Clive to Oliver. 'I see what she means.'

Oliver was out of the car. 'Is that true, Emily? Is Adwoa going with him?'

'Yes—but there's no time to talk about it now. You must stop him before he gets to the works! I saw Tad Fletcher this morning and I know what could happen!'

'You never know what she'll get up to,' Jo muttered.

'Please!' cried Emily. 'Hurry!'

'Okay,' Clive said. 'You hop out, Jo.'

'Hop out? Whatever for?'

'I'd like the women out of the way.'

'*What* did you say ... ?'

'Come on, Jo. Don't waste time,' Oliver said. 'Clive's quite right. Come on. Please. Out.'

Jo got out of the car and Oliver jumped in beside Clive. 'Keep the billy boiling, luv,' he shouted as they moved off. He waved both arms in the air, hanging over the back of the seat and making her a hideous face with squinting eyes and long ears. That could mean *Cheer up* or *Sorry about this* or *Back in ten minutes* . . . She turned slowly, her thoughts bubbling. She was laughing inside herself, laughing and comfortable.

Then she saw Emily's face and everything changed.

'Now, Emily,' she said sharply. 'Don't let's have any of your speciality. There's enough going on already.'

'Yes, all right,' Emily said. 'It's just that I've been wondering all day . . . I've been trying to think. I'm not doing it on purpose, Jo—truly. It's just something left over.'

'I don't know what you're talking about. Left over? Left over from what?'

'From the festival. At Milsom Mag . . .'

'What's left over?' Jo said, chilling in spite of common sense.

'The car. The car on the hill. It's the same car—only it's a different hill. The hill's now. College Hill. The short cut to the works. That's the way they'll go. The way I sent them . . .'

'Don't kid yourself—you're not all that important. Anyone in his senses would go that way.' Jo suddenly broke out, almost shouting, 'You bore me. You're always trying to attract attention . . .' But the roughness and the ugliness died on her and she tried quite deliberately to calm down. 'Look—don't let's get hysterical. It's been a horrible two days, what with Rose and everything. If you're worrying about the Morris—don't. It's in perfect order and anyway Clive drives like a dream.'

Emily turned away and went into the house.

Again rage surged up in Jo and she was all for following Emily, seizing her and shaking her and even slapping her wildly about the face. Then her rage, which she saw was fear, left her and she was calm. She walked briskly out of the gate and stood looking down the road, trying to think what she should do. Of course the car was long out of sight. In the middle of Monday afternoon there was hardly any traffic in this part of the town. What pressure there was would be lower down in the town, where the main coast road crossed the hill . . . The hill. Where there was a notice saying *Accident Black Spot.*

That was when Jo began to run.

Emily knew she had gone. In the empty house she found herself on the floor in the hall, with her face pressed against the sitting-room door. She picked herself up, feeling shamefaced and helpless. Whatever it was she possessed, whatever gift, terrible or otherwise, it was worthless now. She had grown out of it, Kojo had said, and she felt him to be right. Perhaps if she had stayed in Africa, where magic was quite usual, it might have flourished. Here, it was dying. And though she felt the certainty of disaster she was too confused for it to be of any practical use. It had seemed to be of use last year, when she had been so terrified of the festival rally, but how inflated the claim seemed now. Now she only waited for trouble she could not define. As the quiet continued her spirits rose a little, for how easily she might be wrong in her fears.

She heard the front door open and ran into the hall, where Deborah Tower had stopped to glance at the afternoon's post.

'There you are, Emily. Is there any news of Kojo?'

Before Emily could answer, the telephone bell rang; and very far away the donkey-voice of a police siren brayed through the town.

The Tokens

THERE were half a dozen sharp impressions that came out of that day and would not ever be forgotten. The words *Never regained consciousness*, so formal and pompous and true. Clive's immediate cry of 'I've killed him!' and how, even in that moment of time Jo had heard herself cry almost triumphantly, 'It wasn't the Morris! It wasn't the Morris!' In fact it had been the lorry driver, jumping the lights because his brakes had packed up and he had no choice. The Morris was sent careering off into a shop front. There were plenty of witnesses, Kojo and Jo herself among them. The poor old car spun round and accepted the blow nobly on its backside. Clive was not even scratched. Oliver, who was not wearing the seat belt suggestively dangling, was thrown out on his head. Quick and clean, as somebody said. He looked absolutely untouched as Jo ran to help him up, as she had supposed. Somebody grabbed her and moved her out of the way, but she rescued his spectacles from the gutter. He was still alive when they got him to the hospital, but he just didn't wake up. That was when it was said that *He never regained consciousness* and the words went boring away at Jo's mind like a deathwatch beetle in a church roof. She was at home when someone telephoned and told them what had happened at the hospital. Uncle John, it must have been; poor Uncle John.

Jo ran out into the hall when the telephone bell rang, but Emily was ahead of her and snatched up the receiver. 'I'll find him,' she said, without asking who was speaking. And she handed the receiver to David Tower who was already reaching out for it.

Jo and Emily stood side by side. For once it was not difficult for Jo to make a warm, spontaneous gesture and she put her arm round Emily and held her tightly—for already Emily was half inclined to suggest that she was somehow responsible for the disaster. They could tell, of course, from David's replies what had happened.

'Surely they could have done something,' Jo said in a flat, bitter voice. 'They're so clever—they say they're so clever. Surely they could have done *something*.'

'Take it easy, my darling,' she heard her father say—he couldn't have meant to sound so very British. It was so unlike him that she had a hysterical desire to laugh. She felt Emily move away. She went and huddled on the bottom stair and Jo remembered that Oliver had always been her favourite of all the boys. 'Poor Emily,' Jo said. But she could not accept her mother's attempts to hold and comfort her—that softness only turned her to concrete.

'I'd better go and see Aunt Lucy,' she said.

She ran out of the house. It was a lovely evening with a sliver of moon in a pink and blue sky. No wind. A scent of privet gushed from the hedges as she ran by. Even as she felt that the whole world might as well have ended, she knew that all this would be the same next year and the privet would smell just as sweet.

Her uncle, John Evens, opened the door of the house in The Crescent. He always looked frail, but tonight his face seemed skull-like.

'Jo, my dear,' he said. 'How good that you've come.'

'Could I see Aunt Lucy?'

'You know how much she'd like to see you.'

She went into the house. Martin and Simon were standing together in the kitchen doorway and Jo's throat swelled almost to bursting as she saw them so silent. But she ran on into the sitting-room. Perhaps she expected to find Oliver's mother stretched on the sofa with her bitter grief. But she was sitting in the arm-chair by the french windows, a pile of mending on the small table beside her.

'It's got to be done sometime,' she said. 'I'm glad you've come, Jo. I hoped you would. Now I know what I always suspected. We've both lost him, haven't we?'

Jo nodded. She sat down on the arm of the chair and a couple of tears splashed on to her fingers. But she had forced them out and they meant nothing. Oliver's mother did not cry, either. They sat together, she and Jo, and thought about what had happened to them.

Then there were the practical sides to the business. Kojo had witnessed the accident, so he and Adwoa had to wait until after the inquest to make their trip home to Ghana. Adwoa stayed in London and Kojo came back to his room at the David Towers'. He did not go back to the works, so there was no incident. The rather feeble little strike seemed to die of disappointment. The management put new tables into the canteen and promised faith-fully to build more lavatories, so everyone went back to work. Not a coloured face to be seen—except some rather red ones, so Gilbert said.

Then there was the funeral, and so on.

A few days after the winding-up of the affair, Jo went down to the works by herself. She asked George for the key of the shed and he gave it to her quickly, barely looking at her. He was embarrassed, she thought, poor old George, and would have liked to say something but didn't know what. So she took the key and went off to the shed. She unlocked it and slipped inside, pulling the door to behind her. The shed had not been open since the day she went to do the measuring, and the hot sun outside made it almost unbearably stuffy. The polish and splendour of the cars seemed to generate heat as the sun struck them and glinted on brass and chrome and satiny cellulose. On the dry air there was still a hint of her grandmother's scent that Jo had unstoppered the day they brought Paul Darrell to look at the cars.

Jo climbed up into the Bentley and sat, not at the wheel, but in the passenger seat; for in those childish games they had so often played Oliver had most often been the driver. Jo sat there and waited. She had no clear idea what she was waiting for—perhaps for some experience, some understanding that would help her to accept what had happened even though it would not be any easier to bear.

Someone called out, flicking at the barely closed door, 'Who's that in there?'

Jo did not answer. The question was repeated. The door was pushed open and a man came in. It was Tad Fletcher, so Jo called out to him.

'It's me. I'm here.' And she climbed down out of the car and sat as she had so often done on the running board.

'What are you up to, then?' he asked, coming towards her.

'I don't know, really. Looking. Thinking.'

'Ah, don't,' he said, his voice breaking into warmth and understanding, 'don't do it, girl. Don't sit there thinking about that poor lad.'

'I didn't say who I was thinking about.' She laughed a little. 'It's very odd to hear him called a poor lad. He'd bellow with laughter.'

'Poor lad, poor girl—ah, poor Jo Tower,' Tad said, sitting beside her and putting his arm roughly round her shoulders. 'Lass, when I look at you now I don't want my Janet to grow up—we're all happier before we learn to think.'

'What shall I do?' Jo asked him. 'D'you know what I feel like? A widow.' She turned to him, and something in his expression broke down her reserves, unlocked and released her. She put her

head down on his chest and clutched at him and cried as she had
been unable to do for her own mother or for poor Aunt Lucy.
'They think I'm so young and I'll soon get over it, Tad. Shall I?
Shall I?'

'You won't forget, if that's what you mean. Recovery's one
thing—forgetting's something different. You get over losing your
right arm, but you can't forget you had it once. You wouldn't
want to—would you?'

She shook her head. 'No. No. Of course not.'

'You'll move on, that's all,' he said, still holding her firmly,
rocking her a little as if she were a very small child. 'We all do
that, thank God. We all move on, except the dafties. And you're
no daftie, that's certain. Anyway—got things to do, haven't you?'

'I don't know where I'll do them.'

'Here. Where else?'

'It's not Tower Motors any more.'

'It's the works. That's where you want to be, isn't it? And you
want to be there on your own merits. Eh?' Jo nodded furiously.
'Well, of course you do. Then if you're good enough you'll get
where you want, won't you? Like any other chap of us? And
where'd be the sense of coming in to a job you weren't up to—
just because your name was the same? Look, Jo,' Tad said, 'my
boy Ken's coming here. You and he should be asking for jobs
round about the same time. Don't let him beat you to it.'

'Well there you are!' Jo cried, sitting up and smearing at her
face with both hands. '*His* name's the same—the same as yours—
and he'll get the job and I shan't. I *needed* the same name, can't
you see, because people won't take girls seriously.'

'All you need, my girl, is someone to speak up for you when the
time comes. Well—there's Gilbert. There's me.'

'You? Would you? Would you? I'll be good, you know—good
enough for two of us, actually. But I'd better warn you—we all
mean to get together and start a rival firm in time.'

'Do you now.'

'We'll have to begin at the beginning—start from scratch, but

our great-grandfather did that—and there was only one of him.
And even—even without Oliver,' she forced herself to say, 'even
without him we shall be a pretty strong team. I thought I ought
to tell you.'

'Well—thanks,' said Tad. 'That's honest.'

He still had his arm round her shoulders and she was leaning
against him. She remembered Emily saying he'd be a good father.
She was right. Jo began to cry again, but he seemed not to notice,
for he went on talking about the works.

'If I was you lot,' he said, 'I'd rather keep on here. Oh, I know
it's not the same—part of a big concern, a unit. But the pattern's
the same right through, when you come to think of it. I doubt
we'll ever see small private firms like Tower Motors again—well,
small compared with firms like C.M.H. and all those. You start
your new one and put your life and soul into it—it's as likely to be
taken away, just as Tower Motors was taken away from your
Uncle Robert and the rest. It's not only the bosses that count
now, see—it's the shop floor men.'

'Good old Tad,' said Jo grinning.

'Go on—laugh. You're ready to work on the shop floor—you
all say that, don't you? Except that high and mighty youngster of
Mr Miller's—Hugh, is it? Well, then—why can't you chuck out
that bit of family pride that wants it to be *your* floor? It's the work
you're interested in—the sheer noise and power and shine of
machinery. Isn't it? Well—isn't it?'

'Yes.'

'You're not really listening.'

'Yes, I am. Thinking too. I do see what you mean. But I can't
stop wanting it to be us—to be Towers. Okay—family pride.
Only it isn't really pride—well, not vanity, anyway. It's sort of
love . . . Now you're not really listening.'

'I'm listening.' He laughed. 'What made you and me get
off on the wrong foot, eh? What a so-and-so waste of time!'

'I'd feel a bit better if we could just keep the cars,' she said. 'Is
there any news about all that?'

He shook his head. 'Not that I've heard.' Then he gave her a shake and a slap. 'Come on, now. Rouse up, my girl, and do battle.'

'I don't know how.'

'Rubbish. It's your nature. You and I've got many a fine slanging match ahead of us, I shouldn't wonder. I can take it, if you can.'

It was a mighty compliment and she accepted it. 'I can,' she said.

Then she jumped up quickly and went away, leaving him to lock up.

Anthea and Paul wanted to take Jo with them and Emily when they flew back to the States. But she couldn't get herself organised, she said, so no one pushed her. She went to stay with Lydia for a week, and stopped on for nearly a month. The farm rhythms were a good thing and to please Lydia she went riding. Lydia was the best and warmest listener in the world, so they talked a lot about Oliver.

'There were so many of us rushing about the place,' Lydia said. 'I suppose it was too many. Law of averages, and all that.'

Jo went home from Eason Elms in time for Emily's return. At the last minute, in the company of her American aunt, who had turned out magnificently and delighted in being called Aunt Sam, she flew first to Ghana and stayed a night or two with the Amponsahs. She had a lot to talk about when she got home. The Amponsahs topped the list—the new baby's second name was to be Emily.

'Why not her first name?' demanded Jo.

'Because she was born on a Friday, of course,' retorted Emily, 'so her first name is Akua.'

'I see,' said Jo. 'And how's Adwoa getting on?'

'She's nursing at the hospital in Accra. Kojo's got a job with an engineering firm. He's all right now. Perhaps he should never have come here.'

153

'I'm glad he came,' Jo said. 'I expect he did us all some good.'

'He didn't do Rose much good.'

'Yes, he did,' said Jo firmly. 'Rose most of all. Did I tell you when I wrote that she and Auntie Jay have gone to Italy for three weeks? Rose has sent cards all round the family—there's one for you in your room. She sounds pretty gay again. I do hope the Italians can cope with her!'

The first thing Jo had noticed about Emily was that she had grown, and the next was that she had cast off the last faint wisp of orphanhood. She came back to Milsom Parva as to a home she had known for a long time. She rushed to her own room and cried that it was good to be back.

'One thing we must do very soon,' she said to Jo that night, 'is to have a Towering. I don't want to be High Tower any more.'

'Don't you? Why not?'

'Because I was a different me when they made me High Tower. Now I'm what I would have been if I'd been born here in the first place. And if I'd been born here in the first place I don't think I'd have done anything to make me High Tower until I was much older.'

The thought of a Towering alarmed Jo. Oliver would not be there and it would be necessary to draw attention to this fact. Probably Emily would become Martello Tower in his place. Penny would have to be moved up, too, for she was now above Turret age. The name of Dark Tower was free. It did seem as though there was occasion to call the Towering—everyone else seemed in agreement, so Jo and Lydia set about the arrangements as usual.

'Where do you think we should have it, High Tower?'

'Let's think of somewhere where never before,' replied High Tower. 'I had an idea and I got permission. I expect I should have asked you first. In the shed with the old cars. Mr Halliday was as nice as pie.'

Jo looked at her in amazement. 'Travel *does* broaden the mind. I'm stunned. When shall we have it?'

'Saturday week,' said High Tower without hesitation.

That evening was clear but chilly, the last week in September, with a hint of green in the sunset sky to remind of frosts to come. It was not particularly warm in the shed, and not particularly light. Since all the cars were maintained ready for use and their batteries regularly topped up, Robin suggested they should switch on some headlights. The effect was so stunning, so exciting that it took them some time to settle to business.

At last High Tower stood up without first asking Wish Tower or Round Tower, as was usual, and said in a clear and confident voice—'I declare the Towering open.' Then she said, 'First we will pay tribute to Martello Tower.' As she spoke the name the silence knotted itself. High Tower then said: 'Who will pay tribute?'

'I will,' said Wish Tower, very steadily. It had not occurred to her that she would be asked and even less had she imagined volunteering. But she knew it was her place and she would not shirk it. After she had said 'I will', she was silent, collecting herself. 'There is only one tribute needed,' she said at last, in a firm voice. 'I pledge the Towering to remember. That is my tribute from all of us for ever.'

Someone repeated 'For ever'—Roland probably. There was a patter of applause. They were all calm, even the youngest.

There was no faltering in High Tower's handling of the ceremony. She went through her routine easily and confidently. They all knew why they were meeting, so there were no sounds of surprise when she announced that they would now elect a new leader.

'I have made my enquiries,' she said, surprising Jo, but not Lydia, 'and we all have only one candidate. Therefore a vote is unnecessary.' She opened her hand with the Token lying in the palm. 'Towering—with one voice, name High Tower,' she ordered.

'Wish Tower!' came the reply. 'Wish Tower. Wish Tower.'

Now that she had it, Jo did not really want it. She knew it was not necessarily given to console her—but for lots of other acceptable reasons that pleased and warmed her. She took the Token and looked at it on her own palm at last, but she knew that the kick and the will had gone out of the Towering, at least for the present time. It might come again, but it was more likely that something else would take its place—perhaps that working partnership they had so solemnly and purposefully discussed together.

This time Round Tower was left without a partner to do the talking, so after an agonised exchange of raised eyebrows and nudges, she stood up and said in a voice as wavering as if she were addressing a hall full of critical strangers—'I declare the Towering closed.'

Everyone shouted with laughter, and the atmosphere lightened noticeably as Lydia flushed scarlet. They all thought: Oliver would have split his sides—and although no one said it out loud the words seemed to ring on the air.

Emily now sprang up and clapped her hands and called for order. She got up in the seat of the open Mercedes and they all stopped talking again, but rather reluctantly.

'You can't boss us now you're a plain Tower,' someone complained.

'I'm not bossing. I have a pronouncement,' cried Emily. She was very excited. Now it was easy to see that she had got them together for some other reason, besides the Towering.

'Go on, then—pronounce,' Hugh said.

'I have another token. I have another token for High Tower, but she shall hold it for all of us.'

Emily held her closed fist high above her head. Her face was shining and gay. She was confident that she was going to please them, but she wanted to spin out the moment, so she played them and teased them like fish.

Suddenly Jo gave a loud cry. 'Emily! Give it to me! Is it— what I am expecting?'

Then Emily opened her hand. 'A key,' she said. 'I am to hand this key to the Tower of Towers, by instruction from a citizen of a far country!' Then she broke out in wild excitement—'From Paul! From Paul! From rich, kind Paul. He's bought the old cars —and he's sent the key of the shed to the Towering.'

Then the noise within the shed became deafening as they called out and slapped one another, grinning with pleasure as their spirits rose out of melancholy into wild excitement. They ran about among the cars, stroking and patting them, switching the lights on and off in a manner that made Robin groan and call out that all the circuits would be damaged. They danced and shrieked, so that the night watchman came and peered in at them and went away again quickly . . .

Emily had pressed the key into Jo's hand, and she held it tight, along with the Token, warming them both.

'Is it really true?' she asked.

'True as truth,' said Emily. 'That's not the key of this shed, of course. It's the key of the old chapel in Cross Street. That's where we're going to make the museum—and Paul says we've got to make it pay for itself. We'll write it in huge shining letters over the door: *The Tower Transport Museum.*'

'Shall we ask Uncle Saville to be curator? He's sure to be out of a job.'

'He'll have to be good at it,' Emily said severely. 'But if you think he'll be all right—Paul's willing.'

'Come outside a minute,' Jo said. 'I can't hear myself think in here.'

She and Emily went out into the dark, chilly night.

'There's only one thing I want to say, Emily—and you must tell the others because I might make a mess of it. It's a happy ending, isn't it? It really is. In spite of everything, I mean. I'm right, aren't I? Really and truly—it's a different ending, but it's a happy one for all the rest of us. We have to think of that. Haven't we? You say it, Emily—please.'

'All right,' said Emily. 'I mean it, too. It's a happy ending.'

Jo turned and ran back into the shed and the others gathered round her. Everyone had something to say, some idea for the enterprise that would keep the name of Tower still bold and big in the town of Milsom Parva. They began at once, not forgetting they were one short, to make their plans for the future.